Delia couldn't believe what she was thinking. What she was considering.

A vacation fling?

She didn't have flings, vacation or otherwise.

No strings. No attachments. No future. No further expectations. Nothing to answer for.

But here she felt free. Free enough to indulge whatever whim struck her. As if her real self had been left at home while she was in some faraway place where whatever she said or did remained when she returned to her everyday life.

Never before had Delia done more than laugh at the very notion. But now?

Now it seemed to be beckoning to her.

He's a stranger, she reminded herself. *And we're out here, on the beach, in the open.*

It wasn't something Delia McCray did. Ever.

But tonight Delia McCray was back in Chicago, while she—whoever she was at that moment—was here. In paradise…

Dear Reader,

No matter what the weather is like, I always feel like March 1st is the beginning of spring. So let's celebrate that just-around-the-corner thaw with, for starters, another of Christine Rimmer's beloved BRAVO FAMILY TIES books. In *The Bravo Family Way,* a secretive Las Vegas mogul decides he "wants" a beautiful preschool owner who's long left the glittering lights and late nights of Vegas behind. But she hadn't counted on the charms of Fletcher Bravo. No woman could resist him for long….

Victoria Pade's *The Baby Deal,* next up in our FAMILY BUSINESS continuity, features wayward son Jack Hanson finally agreeing to take a meeting with a client—only perhaps he got a little too friendly too fast? She's pregnant, and he's…well, he's not sure what he is, quite frankly. In Judy Duarte's *Call Me Cowboy,* a New York City girl is in desperate need of a detective with a working knowledge of Texas to locate the mother she's never known. Will she find everything she's looking for, courtesy of T. J. "Cowboy" Whittaker? In *She's the One,* Patricia Kay's conclusion to her CALLIE'S CORNER CAFÉ series, a woman who's always put her troublesome younger sister's needs before her own finds herself torn by her attraction to the handsome cop who's about to place said sister under arrest. Lois Faye Dyer's new miniseries, THE McCLOUDS OF MONTANA, which features two feuding families, opens with *Luke's Proposal.* In it, the daughter of one family is forced to work together with the son of the other—with very unexpected results! And in *A Bachelor at the Wedding* by Kate Little, a sophisticated Manhattan tycoon finds himself relying more and more on his Brooklyn-bred assistant (yeah, Brooklyn)—and not just for business.

So enjoy, and come back next month—the undisputed start of spring….

Gail

Please address questions and book requests to:
Silhouette Reader Service
U.S.: 3010 Walden Ave., P.O. Box 1325, Buffalo, NY 14269
Canadian: P.O. Box 609, Fort Erie, Ont. L2A 5X3

THE BABY DEAL

VICTORIA PADE

Silhouette®

SPECIAL EDITION®

Published by Silhouette Books

America's Publisher of Contemporary Romance

Special thanks and acknowledgment are given to
Victoria Pade for her contribution to the
FAMILY BUSINESS series.

 SILHOUETTE BOOKS

ISBN 0-373-24742-7

THE BABY DEAL

Copyright © 2006 by Harlequin Books S.A.

Visit Silhouette Books at www.eHarlequin.com

Printed in U.S.A.

Books by Victoria Pade

Silhouette Special Edition

VICTORIA PADE

is a native of Colorado, where she continues to live and work. Her passion—besides writing—is chocolate, which she indulges in frequently and in every form. She loves romance novels and romantic movies—the more lighthearted, the better—but she likes a good, juicy mystery now and then, too.

Chapter One

White sandy beaches. Crystal-clear water washing over coral reefs. Lush, dense foliage below enormous palm trees. Soft, lilting music. The scent of sea and soil and sweet, sweet flowers wafting on a balmy breeze.

Paradise.

Tahiti really was paradise, Delia McCray thought as she looked out over the small table where she sat.

The last night of her vacation.

A trio of Polynesians played guitar, ukulele and drums to one side of the wooden dance floor, where her half brother Kyle and his wife, Janine, and Kyle's and Delia's half sister Marta and Marta's husband, Henry, swayed to the sounds.

Delia smiled at the sight. The five-day trip had been

her treat, a reward for everyone's hard work. It was also her own first vacation in ten years—so it wasn't something she'd done lightly—and it was heartening to see how much everyone was enjoying it.

Despite the fact that the three McCray children weren't full-blooded siblings, they'd been raised by the mother they'd shared and they were close. They'd always looked out for each other, and it was nice that they'd been able to have this time together. Even if Delia was aware of being odd man out at moments like this when the two couples paired up.

Her focus settled on Kyle, who was holding Janine close and saying something to her that made her laugh. Delia had no idea what he'd said, but she smiled, too, warmed even from a distance by what they shared.

Kyle was the baby of the family at twenty-eight and Delia couldn't help feeling proud of him, of the man he was. The man he'd made of himself in a houseful of women.

Kyle was un-tall, as he liked to say, but he was lean and wiry, and while he had Delia's same white-blond hair, his hazel eyes and ruddier skin color were more like Marta's.

Marta, who danced into Delia's view just then and diverted her attention, was the middle child at thirty-two.

As Delia watched, Marta pressed her cheek to the shoulder of her husband, Henry. Henry laid his cheek atop Marta's short-cropped black curls, and his hands dropped lovingly to his wife's curvaceous hips.

It wasn't any surprise that no one ever guessed that

Delia and Marta were sisters. They looked nothing alike. Marta's nose was a bit hooked at the end, while Delia's was turned up. Marta's eyes were a mishmash of brown and green, while Delia's were decidedly blue. Marta's lips were fuller, Delia's skin was much more pale, and they'd never been able to trade bras because Delia couldn't even begin to fill one of Marta's. But despite the external differences, they were soul mates.

"You could be out there dancing, too…"

Delia smiled at the deep voice that came from behind her, feeling the scant brush of breath against the ear her very straight, blunt-cut shoulder-length hair was tucked around.

Andrew.

"I could be out there dancing if I had a partner," she countered, braver and more flirtatious than she would ever have been if she were home in Chicago. Or without the liquid courage provided by the sour-apple martinis she'd been drinking.

Andrew came around to set a tray full of fresh drinks on the table and—again under the influence of the liquor that was making her head light—Delia's gaze went unabashedly to the man she'd only met the day before. He was handsome enough to cause even the splendor of paradise to fade into the background.

Andrew.

She knew him only as that, since they hadn't ex-changed last names. He was tall, at least six feet, with broad shoulders, a strong back and pure, solid muscle, the only bulk he carried.

His hair was a sun-streaked light brown and he wore it a bit long on top.

His face was an interesting combination of refined features and a touch of ruggedness that carved the edges of his jaw and his nose into sharp angles. His brow was square. His cheekbones were pronounced. His lips were slightly on the thin side and his eyes were so dark a shade of brown they were the color of Columbian coffee beans.

With looks like his, he seemed to be the kind of man who would squire models on each arm and not fraternize with lesser mortals, yet since they'd met he hadn't appeared to notice any of the women who had ogled him. He'd just fit in as one of the guys—one of the McCrays—and if he were aware of how he put height-challenged Kyle and paunchy Henry to shame, he didn't show any sign of it.

Or maybe he was just so comfortable with his own striking good looks that he forgot about them. Anything was possible, Delia conceded, acknowledging to herself that she didn't actually know anything about Andrew except that he was good company and had been able to tell them where the best spot on the island was to snorkel.

He'd arrived at the resort the day before, had overheard them talking at dinner the previous evening about their plans for their last day in Tahiti and he'd offered his advice. And since he was apparently as familiar with their surroundings as any native, when he'd also offered to show them the spot he'd suggested, they'd taken him up on it and spent the day with him.

As thanks for his guidance, the McCrays had invited him to have dinner with them. And now here they were, at the palapa—the open-air bar and dance area covered by a thatched roof only a few yards from the water— savoring the last few hours of their final evening in Tahiti.

Well, the McCrays' final evening. Andrew wasn't leaving.

He was, however, holding out a hand to Delia just then.

"I'd love to be your dance partner," he said with a smile that flashed perfect white teeth and created a dimple at the left corner of his mouth.

"You don't have to," Delia demurred, some of her bravery flagging suddenly.

"I do, though," he insisted. "These are my dancing shoes."

His own dark eyes dropped to his feet and Delia's followed, albeit somewhat slower as her glance drifted down his taut, polo-shirted torso to his narrow waist, to hips caressed by khaki slacks, to thighs thick enough to hint at their existence within his pant legs.

He was wearing deck shoes, not dancing shoes— without socks—and Delia had to quell a tiny shiver of something that almost felt like arousal at the sight of nothing more than a fraction of an inch of naked foot between the vamp of his shoes and the break of his slacks.

At home, deck shoes and no socks would have been a turnoff. But then at home she also wouldn't have been in nothing more than a tight, spaghetti-strapped camisole that she usually only wore underneath things, a brightly colored sarong tied at her waist over her bikini bottoms and sandals. But she wasn't at home. She was in Tahiti. On vacation.

And anything goes, she thought.

Andrew was still holding out his hand to her, waiting for her to take it, to accept his invitation to dance.

"Come on," he said in a deep voice that tempted and cajoled at once.

Why not? Delia asked herself, taking the plunge. And his hand. And getting to her feet at the same moment Andrew's extremely handsome face erupted into a grin.

"Good girl! I knew you had it in you," he praised, teasing her.

He led her to the dance floor and swung her into his arms. The movement sent Delia's head spinning, warning her that she really was already under the influence of alcohol.

It didn't matter, though. Not when she felt so good. Not when everything seemed right with the world.

Marta gave her a thumbs-up over Henry's shoulder when she caught Delia's eye, bestowing sisterly approval and encouragement of Delia letting down her hair—an uncommon occurrence.

Delia only smiled in return as Andrew pulled her closer and proved he was as adept at dancing as he'd been at everything else they'd done today.

And it was nice. Nice not to be odd man out anymore. Nice to feel a man's strong arms around her—something that hadn't happened in a long, long while. Nice to be where she was, who she was, with her family and this very pleasant, personable stranger. Nice to be oh-so-relaxed and fancy-free, with nothing to do but have a little fun. Nice, for once, to just go with the flow....

And that was exactly what Delia did for the remainder of the evening. She danced with Andrew and Henry and Kyle. She drank more—and more—sour-apple martinis. She laughed and flirted and had a good time until one by one the other people in the palapa disappeared. Until Kyle and Janine wandered off to their bungalow. Until Marta and Henry wandered off to theirs.

Until Delia was left all alone with Andrew, on the dance floor yet again.

His arms were slung low on her hips. His hands were clasped together at the small of her back. Her arms were hooked over his shoulders. Her brow was against the wall of his chest. His chin was on the crown of her head. And they were barely swaying to the lazy strains of a very slow song.

"Why is it that vacations take so long to get here and then end so soon?" she lamented in a singsongy, dreamy voice.

Above her, Andrew chuckled a throaty chuckle that was all male. "I don't believe in ever letting them take too long to get here," he said. "And who says it has to end? You could change your plans. Stay…"

Delia laughed. She sounded giddy to her own ears but she didn't care. "Stay?"

"You could send Kyle and Janine and Marta and Henry on their way and stay," Andrew said. And unless Delia was mistaken, he was serious.

She lifted her head from his chest to peer up at that face that was too good to believe. "I can't stay," she said, *not* sounding serious even though she was.

"Sure you can. A few phone calls can arrange anything. I know the owner of this resort—I stay here often. I'll get him to let you keep your bungalow. And I'll be here…."

That last part was the real enticement.

Again Delia laughed. "No, no, no," she said unfirmly.

"Yes, yes, yes," he responded, dipping forward enough to press a kiss to the spot just above her ear.

The kiss surprised her. He hadn't done anything like that before. But somehow it didn't shock her. Or put her off. It was just another thing that seemed nice. And tantalizing. Like him.

"No, no, no," she repeated, still not strongly and not even sure herself whether she was saying no to his suggestion that she remain in Tahiti or to that kiss. But either way, it didn't have enough force to mean much.

"A few more days—what harm could it do?"

Delia laughed. "Don't ask me hard questions after I've had so many martinis."

It was Andrew's turn to laugh. He also squeezed her enough to bring her closer still to the solid wall of his body. "I'll miss you if you go."

He made that sound genuine even though Delia doubted it was true.

"I think you'll probably survive the horrors of Tahiti without me," she said facetiously.

"But at what cost?" he asked with a voice full of mock drama, making her laugh again.

The bartender had been working at closing the bar for a while and had apparently finished his tasks, because he stepped from behind it to leave just as the last strains of music came to an end.

"That's all for tonight," the ukulele player announced in French-accented English, and the trio picked up and followed the bartender.

But Andrew didn't pay them any attention. His gaze never wavered from Delia, and he went on swaying as if there were still something to sway to.

"I think we've closed the place," Delia whispered as if it were a confidence, meeting his coffee-colored eyes with her own.

Andrew merely smiled a small, contented smile and then dipped down to kiss her again. This time on the lips. A soft, soft kiss that sent tiny tingles raining through her as if it were midnight on New Year's Eve and someone had just dropped a handful of confetti over her.

He stopped kissing her but the tingles lingered.

"Does this mean our night has to end?" he asked, his voice suddenly so deep it was nearly inaudible.

Delia glanced around at the empty tables, the abandoned bar, the drum set left deserted, and then looked up at Andrew again. Only as she did, she became aware of just how much she *didn't* want this night to be over quite yet.

"We could take a walk on the beach," she suggested.

Another smile spread across his supple mouth, slow and lazy and pleased.

"Better than nothing," he said, swaying a few minutes more before finally bringing their semblance of dancing to a halt.

He caught one of her hands in his to hold as they left the palapa and headed towards the surf.

Delia had no idea what time it was. But as they passed the bungalows—all of them over-water bamboo bungalows with palm-thatch roofs that could only be reached by crossing a wooden bridge to a dock that connected them—she couldn't see a single light on anywhere. No signs of life appeared on the beach itself, either, making it seem as if she and Andrew were the only two people on the entire island.

There was just the sound of the calm sea lapping gently at the shore as Andrew took her near the water's edge and headed away from the bungalows beneath a sky spotted with stars paying homage to an almost full moon.

They didn't talk. They just walked.

Ordinarily a silence like that would have made Delia uncomfortable. But there, then, it didn't. Instead she was absorbed in details like the length of Andrew's legs, the confidence of his stride even on the wet sand, the warm strength of his hand around hers and how much she liked it. All of it. All of him.

The bungalows were only dots far in the distance when they stopped. Shoes were kicked off and they sat on the dry portion of the beach—Andrew behind Delia, his arms wrapping her as if it were something they'd done a million times before.

"Maybe if I just hang on tight and don't let go of you you'll stay," he said, his mouth close to her ear, his voice intimate.

"Can't stay," she repeated, allowing her head to fall back to his shoulder.

To accomplish that, her head was tilted to one side and Andrew pressed a kiss to her neck, sighing a resigned and disappointed-sounding sigh that bathed her skin in a hot gust of breath.

"I guess we'd better make tonight last, then," he said.

Delia wasn't sure what he meant by that. But she knew what was going through her own mind. Although she didn't know why or where it had come from.

What was going through her own mind were thoughts of indeed making tonight last.

In this man's arms...

She couldn't believe what she was thinking. What she was considering.

A vacation fling?

She didn't have flings, vacation or otherwise.

Not that it was unheard of to her. She had a friend who loved telling stories of holiday romances. A friend who didn't consider vacations a success unless she met someone to flirt with, to have fun with, someone to send her home with memories that put secret smiles on her face....

No strings. No attachments. No future. No further expectations. Nothing to answer for.

That was what Delia's friend said was part of the allure. Just a fling at a time when she felt free. Free enough to indulge whatever whim struck her. As if her real self had been left at home while she was in some faraway place where whatever she said or did remained there when she returned to her everyday life….

Never before, when Delia's friend had talked about it, had Delia done more than laugh at the very notion. But now?

Now it seemed to be beckoning to her.

Just a vacation fling …

Throw caution to the wind, her friend's voice seemed to say in the breeze.

Andrew was tugging on her earlobe with tender teeth, flicking the edge with the tip of his tongue and setting off more of that confetti tingling through her.

He's a stranger, she reminded herself. *And we're out here, on the beach, in the open...*

It wasn't something Delia McCray did. *Ever.*

But tonight she really did have the sense that Delia McCray was back in Chicago, while she—whoever she was at that moment—was here. In paradise. With this broad-shouldered, suntanned, muscled man who was nibbling her jawline even as her nipples grew to taut little knots against his forearm and he pushed back on them to let her know he felt it, too.

He uncrossed his legs from where they'd been at her derriere and stretched one on either side of her, coming up closer behind her. Close enough for her to know his thoughts were on the same course that hers were.

He wanted her. There was unmistakable proof. And

knowing it erupted a whole flood of desires in Delia that she didn't even know she was capable of. Overwhelming desires. Driving needs that demanded their due…

She'd had too much to drink. She knew it. She knew it as well as she knew she wasn't completely in her right mind.

But she wanted this man as much as he so obviously wanted her. She wanted this moment. This vacation fling.

She tilted her head and turned it as far as she could to see Andrew out of the corner of her eye. Realizing all over again how handsome he was gilded in moonglow.

She smiled.

And she flexed her hips firmly back into him.

He smiled, too. An answering kind of smile that said he knew. He understood. A smile so sexy she could hardly stand it.

Then one of his hands came to her breast, engulfing it, grasping it, making her nipple stand at attention in his palm so forcefully she thought that small kernel might actually burst right through the negligible containment of the spandex camisole just to have the unbridled feel of his skin against it.

He craned forward enough to cover her mouth with his. His lips were parted. His tongue wasn't shy in the slightest. And in one motion he turned her toward him.

Her sarong came untied and fell away but she didn't care. She was far more interested in reaching her arms around him, in giving herself over to him completely, in shedding any inhibitions that might have been lurking and allowing everything her body was crying out for to be answered.

There.

Right out in the open.

On that Tahitian beach.

Under the watchful eye of nothing but the moon.

Chapter Two

Monday morning. Bright and early. Or funds to your account are stopped. I'm not kidding.

It was Monday morning. 8:00 a.m. And Andrew Hanson was where he'd been ordered to be. Ordered via e-mail by his older brother Jack. Complete with the threat that if he didn't show up at the Chicago offices of Hanson Media Group, he would be financially cut off from all future support by family funds.

So there he was. Only hours off a plane from Tahiti. Barely showered. Unshaven. Dressed in jeans and a T-shirt. And wishing for eight hours sleep. Wishing even more to be back on the beach he'd been on for the last three months. Or on any other beach for that matter.

It was a common response for him. Especially

whenever anything on the home front got complicated or unpleasant or became a drag. And things in Chicago at that moment were complicated, unpleasant *and* a drag. The death of his father had caused all of that at once three months ago, and so as soon as the funeral was over Andrew had done what he had done frequently in the past—he'd hightailed it out of town to wherever seemed like the best escape, Tahiti, this time. Tahiti, where he'd fully intended to stay for a long, long while.

A long, long while that wouldn't have ended, except that after ignoring numerous e-mails from his older brother and their uncle David—their late father's much younger brother—Jack had forced Andrew to come back to Chicago.

To help with the recent disasters that had befallen Hanson Media Group, the family business.

A woman Andrew assumed to be a receptionist or a secretary had shown him to the conference room, informing him that Jack and David would be with him soon. But he had no idea how soon *soon* was and he really needed some sleep, so he plopped down on one of the chairs at the large table and used a second chair for his feet. Then he let his head fall to the back of the chair he was sitting in and closed his eyes.

But despite the fact that he was tired and jet-lagged and could usually doze off anywhere without any problem, he didn't doze off now.

He just couldn't stop thinking, *What the hell do Jack and David think* I *can do…?*

Hanson Media Group was in trouble. That much

Andrew knew. Apparently his father, George—who had run the media conglomerate—had not been as savvy a businessman as he'd led everyone to believe. As savvy a businessman as George's and David's own father, who had built Hanson Media Group from the ground up.

But rather than exposing his failings to his family, George had kept two sets of books—one that made him look good and another that told the truth. The truth being that he'd run Hanson Media Group—the source of the wealth that had always supported all the Hanson family—into the ground. To the verge of bankruptcy.

Jack had temporarily stepped in after George's death and discovered the second set of books. Now he and David were in the process of giving it their all to turn things around. But compounding matters, one of Jack's attempts had led to the Internet portion of Hanson Media Group inadvertently being linked to a pornography site that had stirred further trouble for the company with morality groups.

Jack's and David's e-mails had kept Andrew up-to-date on these matters, so Andrew was well aware of the dire situation. He just didn't have any idea why his brother and his uncle thought it was so crucial that he be here in the middle of it, too.

The sound of his brother's voice coming from just outside the conference room alerted Andrew to Jack's imminent arrival. It caused Andrew to open his eyes but not to sit up or even to take his feet off the other chair.

Within moments the door opened and in strode Jack

and David, both in business clothes and looking far more professional than Andrew did.

Andrew saw the other men take note of his casual attire but neither of them said anything.

"Finally," was what Jack did say, clearly in reference to Andrew's belated attendance, his impatience with Andrew ringing in his voice.

"Hi, guys," Andrew greeted in return.

Jack shook his head in disgust and sat across the conference table from him.

David offered a tight smile. "Good to see you, Andrew. We're glad you're here."

"Good to see you, too, big D. I'm just not sure why I *am* here," Andrew responded, cutting to the chase in hopes that this meeting could be quick and he could get back to his apartment for some sleep.

Jack had gone to business school, and to law school as well. Before George's death Jack had been a practicing attorney with ambitions of becoming a judge. Now it struck Andrew that his brother was sitting as stiff-backed as if he were already on the bench.

Jack had brought in several files and now he set them on the table and slid them across to Andrew with a force that sent them sailing to the edge.

Andrew didn't raise so much as a finger to intercept them and if they hadn't stopped on their own they would have ended up on the floor.

"You're here to go to work," Jack announced unceremoniously then.

It wasn't like Jack to make jokes but that struck Andrew as funny. "Work?" he repeated.

"Work," his older brother confirmed.

David, who had always stood up for his nephews, took a more friendly tone as he sat at the head of the table where Andrew could see him without so much as turning his head.

"We need your help, Andrew. The porn scandal caused more problems. That computer hacker who fixed it so that people—even kids—who were surfing our Web pages could inadvertently be switched to a pornographic site nearly did us in. We're still trying to recover, to convince people that it *was* the hacker who did it, that Hanson Media Group has absolutely no affiliation with pornography in any way, shape or form. But we've lost advertisers and that means we've lost revenue we couldn't afford to lose. So we had to lay off a lot of people just to continue making payroll once we realized what financial shape Hanson Media Group is in. We're down manpower—"

"And if you want money from the company you're going to have to earn it," Jack cut in, finishing what David was saying and sounding every bit the big brother who was put out with his younger sibling.

"What can I possibly do?" Andrew asked. "I don't have a clue about what goes on here."

"No, you just cash the checks," Jack said, brusquely.

"We're trying to get hold of Evan, too," David added as if to let Andrew know he wasn't the only errant Hanson being asked to pitch in. "But Evan is being even worse than you were about answering our calls and e-mails," David concluded with a tone that showed his irritation.

Evan was the middle brother—five years Jack's

junior, two years older than Andrew. Evan was more like Andrew in his freewheeling ways and lifestyle than he was the nose-to-the-grindstone, judicious Jack, or their straight-arrow uncle. But Andrew was a little surprised that he'd caved before Evan had.

He didn't say that, though. Instead, still without reaching for the manila folders or claiming them in any way, Andrew cast his brother a dismissive gaze to let Jack know he wasn't taking any guff from him, and then focused on his uncle once more as David said, "We want you to sell advertising. We're hurting badly on that front and—"

"And it mainly involves wining and dining clients and potential clients so we figured that wasn't too far removed from your good-time-Charlie talents," Jack said, completing David's thought for the second time.

"I may know about wining and dining, but advertising? Like I said, not a clue," Andrew insisted, still half wondering if they were joking.

But when his uncle clasped his hands together, laid them on the table and leaned forward, Andrew knew that wasn't the case.

"Look, Andy," David said earnestly. "We need you. There just isn't a choice anymore. We're short-staffed and the only money Hanson Media Group can afford to let out of here has to go to people producing for the company."

"In other words," Jack added, "there are no more free lunches. You can work for Hanson Media Group or you can get a job somewhere else, but one way or another you're going to have to earn a living."

Andrew might not have finished college but he wasn't stupid. He knew he didn't have anything to offer when it came to the job market. But he still wasn't sure his brother and his uncle weren't overestimating his abilities.

"It's not that I'm not sympathetic," he said. "Or that I'm not willing to reduce my living expenses or whatever. But I'm not a high-pressure salesman."

"You'll learn," David assured as if he had every confidence in him. "Jack and I will walk you through things until you get the hang of it all. But you're personable. Likable. You make friends easily. You wow the women without even trying. You can talk to anyone and put them at ease, make them comfortable and open to your ideas, your suggestions. Those things go a long way in sales. That's why we know you can do this."

"I'm glad you think so," Andrew said under his breath.

"You really can do this," Jack said then, curbing some of the attitude he'd been displaying since coming into the conference room. "It'll be right up your alley. You'll just have to put some effort into it."

"*Effort* meaning wear a suit and show up here every day—nine to five? Go to meetings? Do paperwork? Call clients? That sort of thing?"

"Your office is right down the hall," David said as if he were thrilled and relieved that Andrew was on board, when Andrew didn't actually feel as if he'd *agreed* to be on board yet.

"And it won't always be just nine to five," Jack

amended. "For instance, tonight you and I are having dinner with a company called Meals Like Mom's."

David picked up the ball and ran with it from there. "Last month Meals Like Mom's made the list of top-ten up-and-coming businesses in the Chicago area. It's an innovative concept that's taking off. Healthy, nutritious, preservative-free meals can be purchased at reasonable costs either from a few specialty shops or delivered right to people's houses. Busy, working parents can put a dinner on the table for their whole family that looks and tastes like they've spent the day cooking. Or single people or couples can treat themselves to a well-balanced, great-tasting meal without any hassle. Or Meals Like Mom's will send in a hundred or more boxed lunches—we did it on the larger scale at the last board meeting. All with the guarantee that the food will taste like someone has prepared it especially for them, like their Mom would make."

"Okay," Andrew said, only half paying attention.

His uncle continued. "My eyes and ears in the advertising world tell me that Meals Like Mom's has just hired one of the biggest local agencies to do commercials, radio spots and print ads for them. That's all going to have to go somewhere and it might as well be to Hanson Media Group. They could be a huge account for us and they could also bring with them the kind of clean image we need to be connected with right now."

"All the information we have on the Meals Like Mom's organization is in one of those files," Jack said. "You'll need to read it, become familiar with it. The other file will show you the deal we're offering and how it compares—favorably—with other local media outlets. That's something you'll want to use as a selling point. The third file will fill you in on what you're to say should the subject of the porn scandal come up—that could well be a sore spot for a company with *Mom* in the title. The meeting is at six. The restaurant's name and address are on a Post-it in one of the files. I'll meet you there at five forty-five. Suit and tie. Clean shaven. And get your hair trimmed. You look like someone who's been laying on a beach for months."

Without waiting for a reply, Jack stood and walked to the conference room door.

But he paused there to glance back at Andrew. "Welcome to the real world. Time to grow up, little brother."

And out he went, leaving Andrew alone with David.

But if Andrew had any hope of his uncle softening the blow he'd just been dealt, it didn't come.

David stood, too. "Read through the files, commit everything to memory and then go out and get yourself fixed up and dress for tonight. This is important."

Andrew didn't respond. He just stared at his uncle.

David passed by him on his way to the door, patted his shoulder and said, "I know you're up to this, Andy. I have faith in you."

Andrew merely raised his chin in acknowledgement of that, not wanting to say his uncle's faith might be unwarranted.

Then David said, "Let me see if your office is ready for you and I'll show you to it, introduce you around."

And out he went, too, leaving Andrew once again alone in the conference room.

Which was probably a good thing since the expletive he muttered wouldn't have been well-received had anyone been there to hear it.

Sales? he silently shrieked to himself. They wanted him to be a salesman? To sell advertising? He didn't know squat about selling *or* advertising. Or about having an office he had to show up at every day. In a suit and tie.

He voiced another, even more colorful expletive under his breath.

This was the last thing he'd figured he was coming home to. He'd thought Jack and David might have wanted to liquidate portions of the company's holdings, or consolidate things, or that maybe they'd wanted to fill him in on legalities that had arisen out of the porn scandal. He'd figured that there was just something they wanted him to pretend an interest in, to lend his support to. Some kind of family-unity thing or something.

But putting him to work? He hadn't even considered that that was a possibility. Hell, he'd never worked for the company. Or for anyone else. All his life Hanson Media Group had just done its thing and he'd done his, thrilled to have his share of the proceeds deposited in his account every month.

And now those days were over.

He didn't like it.

But whether he liked it or not, whether he liked the idea of being an advertising salesman or not, whether he could do it or not, apparently didn't make a difference. Jack and David were set on this and clearly he didn't have a choice in the matter. Not if he wanted to continue to have an income. And what would he do *without* an income?

He was stuck. And he knew it. With nothing to do but comply.

For now, anyway.

Because maybe those good old days weren't really over. Maybe they were just suspended for the time being. Maybe before too long things would turn around. The scandal would blow over. Business would pick up. Former employees could be rehired. And he could just go back to the life he'd been living.

It helped to think that that might be a possibility—even if there hadn't been anything in any of what his brother or his uncle had said to lead him to believe it. It helped to think that this wasn't permanent. It made it all the more easy to accept that way. In fact, it was the only way he *could* accept it at that moment.

So he sighed, hung on to the notion that this would have a limited run, and finally conceded that he was going to have to sell advertising. At least for a while. And he reached for the files on the table, bringing them to his lap.

Files.

This was *so* not him....

But still he opened the one on top, knowing only when he did which file he was looking at first.

Meals Like Mom's—it was the background information on the company he was supposed to recruit tonight.

Just below the name of the company was the owner's name—Delia McCray.

Andrew took a closer look at that, thinking his eyes and his overwhelmed brain were playing tricks on him.

But no, he'd read it right the first time—the name was Delia.

"Huh," he mused.

Delia wasn't a common name. And now here he was, encountering it twice—three months ago in Tahiti and again today.

Maybe the universe was toying with him, he thought. Because the Delia he'd met in Tahiti had sort of haunted him, and just when he was regretting the fact that he'd heeded Jack's and David's e-mails and left the island, he was reminded of Tahiti and Tahiti Delia all over again.

Tahiti Delia…

Oh, yeah, Tahiti Delia had definitely stuck with him even after she'd left him on the beach at sunrise the morning after they'd spent the night together.

Flaxen hair that was so pale a blond it was like lemons diluted with cream. Flawless porcelain skin that could have been the envy of newborn babies. A small nose that was a little pointed at the end where it gracefully curved up just the slightest. High, high cheekbones that gave her beautiful face a fragile look. Lips that were thin but coy and sexy, too. And oh, man, what eyes she'd had—eyes the color of crystal-clear ocean waves just before they broke against the shore.

Eyes that were a blue like no other. Glistening and shimmering and capable of sweeping a person right off his feet.

Top it all off with long, lanky legs that had seemed to go on forever despite the fact that she hadn't been too tall, a tight rear end and just enough up front, and Tahiti Delia had been something dreams were made of.

And he'd had plenty of dreams of her and their tryst under the stars, there was no mistake about that. Plenty of dreams that had let him relive their encounter, that had left him aching to do it all over again. That had made him sorry that they'd had only that one night…

"Ready to see your new digs?"

Andrew had been so lost in thoughts of Tahiti Delia he hadn't heard his uncle return to the conference room door to poke his head in.

As if he were guilty of something, Andrew yanked his feet off the chair and stood, fumbling with the files he'd forgotten about and nearly dropped, before he snatched them up to take with him.

"Yeah. Sure," he muttered, sounding as distracted as he felt and trying hard to get himself out of that daydream and back to reality.

Trying, too, to find some kind of work mindset and wondering—when a wave of what felt like claustrophobia hit him—whether he was actually going to be able to pull off holding this job.

Especially when it took so little to carry him back to Tahiti.

And to Tahiti Delia.

Chapter Three

"We'll give him five more minutes and then if he isn't here, we'll go on without him. And again, I can't apologize enough. But as I said, he was just back from vacation today, I dumped a whole lot on him that he hadn't expected, he was jet-lagged, hadn't slept and—"

"Honestly," Delia assured Jack Hanson, "we understand. Your brother is only ten minutes late. It's not a problem."

The tight smile that the acting head of Hanson Media Group gave to Delia, Marta and Gwen—the ad agent handling their account—was enough to let Delia know that regardless of what Jack Hanson said, his brother was in for it when he got him alone after this dinner meeting.

But just then Jack Hanson's expression eased and he said, "Here he is."

They had already been seated at a round table in the restaurant Gwen had suggested and since Delia's back was to the door, she took Jack Hanson's word for it and didn't crane around to see for herself. Neither did Marta—also sitting without easy access. But Gwen obviously saw the approach of the other Hanson brother and seemed to like what she saw, because the smile that had begun as businesslike became something else entirely. At the same time her eyes widened and she sat up taller in her chair, drawing her shoulders back in a way that pushed out her ample chest.

And then Jack Hanson's brother came around the table to the vacant chair that had been left for him. Where Delia and Marta could both see him.

"Oh!" Marta exclaimed as Delia merely peered up in sudden shock.

"Andrew!" Marta added then. "It's Andrew! From Tahiti."

"Delia?" he said, his focus omitting Marta and everyone else at the table as his espresso eyes honed in on Delia. "I saw your name in the file but... You're Delia *McCray?*"

"You all know each other?" Jack asked.

"Sort of," Delia answered, struggling to find her voice and some aplomb to go with it. "We just met— briefly—in Tahiti. When Marta and I and the rest of our family were there. A few months ago."

A million things were popping into Delia's mind suddenly. This was not a situation or a scenario she'd ever imagined. And in the last month and a half she'd imagined many.

To her rapidly increasing dismay, rather than taking his chair, Andrew came back around the table to press a kiss to her cheek. A kiss that was nothing, considering the night they'd spent together. But a kiss that unnerved her even further. A kiss she barely tilted her head to receive.

"It's great to see you!" Andrew said. Then, raising his chin to Marta, he added, "You, too, Marta. I just can't believe it."

"Small world," Gwen contributed as if to remind them of her presence.

"And this is Gwen Davis, the account executive from DeWit and Sheldon—the ad agency handling Meals Like Mom's," Jack said to include the other woman.

"Oh, I'm sorry, Gwen," Delia apologized. "Of course. This is Gwen. Gwen, this is Andrew…Hanson?" Since Delia was only assuming that was Andrew's last name she had to add a questioning inflection at the end of that.

"That's me, Andrew Hanson," Andrew confirmed, holding out a hand to Gwen before he returned to take his seat. And to staring at Delia. "Delia. I still can't believe this."

The waiter arrived with the wine Jack had ordered and after getting his approval for the selection, the waiter began pouring glasses of the ruby-hued brew. Delia's mind was spinning in a private panic and when the waiter reached her it was Marta who snatched Delia's glass out of the way.

"No wine for our mom-to—" Marta cut her own words short, gasping as if that might reclaim them.

And Delia cringed inside, hoping and praying that no one would finish Marta's phrase.

But her hopes and prayers were for naught.

"Mom-to-*be?*" Gwen asked. "Is that what you were going to say, Marta?" But before Marta could respond, Gwen looked to Delia and said, "Are you pregnant?"

It crossed Delia's mind to say no, she wasn't pregnant. To try to connect her sister's comment to the name of her business somehow. But not only couldn't she come up with a way to do that, it also occurred to her that it was futile, that she'd be working with Gwen and possibly with the Hansons, and that there wouldn't be any concealing the pregnancy before long, that it would seem silly that she'd denied it when it was true. So she opted for forging ahead.

"Yes," she answered quietly.

Marta leaned over and whispered, "Go ahead, shoot me now."

But Delia merely forced a semblance of a smile. She couldn't blame her sister for something that had happened naturally. Delia, Marta and Kyle had always been watchdogs for each other, and since Delia had discovered that she was pregnant, Marta had been doing things like that whenever she and Delia were together. Delia knew it was a reflex by now. It was just that ordinarily they were in private when it happened and for this to be the first public announcement couldn't have been worse timing.

"Well, congratulations!" Gwen said as if the news pleased her more than there was any reason for it to.

"So Meals Like Mom's is really going to have a mom," Jack pointed out. "Congratulations."

"Thank you. All around," Delia said, fighting mortification and wishing Andrew would stop boring into her with the gaze she was trying not to return.

"Pregnant?"

Andrew muttered so quietly it was barely audible. Which was good because it left Delia hoping no one else had picked up on the personal note she could have sworn she heard in his voice.

Just when she didn't think this could get any worse, Gwen said, "When are you due?"

Now that she'd come this far in the forging-ahead department, she could hardly stop by refusing to answer a perfectly common question. Even if it did feel as if she were exposing herself even more. But the best she could do was a barely audible, "Six months."

Her sister jumped in. "But that isn't what we came here to talk about tonight, is it?" Marta said, her own voice a touch too bright and an octave higher than it should have been. "We came to discuss advertising and we've put it off long enough."

"My fault," Andrew said.

Delia's glance went involuntarily to him at that, unsure for a split second what he was confessing to.

But then he continued. "I promise to make amends for keeping you all waiting."

"Waiting. Right," Delia said in relief. "Well, let's not wait any longer," she said and ushered them into talking business, counting on Marta to pay close attention because just making it through this dinner was going to be about as much as Delia could pull off. She knew she wasn't going to retain a word that was said about anything from then on.

Not now that the cat was out of the bag.

To a man she'd been absolutely sure she'd never see again.

"Why don't you and I discuss a few more things over a drink at the bar?"

It was Gwen Davis's suggestion to Andrew when the dinner meeting was concluded and everyone had stood to leave. Gwen had been less than subtle all through the meal, making it clear that she wanted to get to know Andrew better. On a personal level.

Delia had repeatedly reminded herself that there was no reason for her to feel anything whatsoever about that. That she had no hold over Andrew. That he'd been nothing but a vacation fling for her. She'd also told herself that it shouldn't matter to her under any circumstances. Not even her current ones.

But Gwen's interest in Andrew still irked Delia to no end.

So it was satisfying when Andrew rejected the advance.

But it was less satisfying and far more stress inducing when he then hung back, took Delia's arm to draw her nearer, and said close to her ear, "Actually, I was hoping to persuade you to have a cup of coffee with me. Alone. I thought we could catch up. Talk…"

Feeling as if she couldn't refuse, Delia said a reluctant, "All right."

Marta had overheard the exchange and with the same apologetic expression that had been on her face every time she'd looked at Delia since the comment that had revealed Delia's pregnancy, she said, "Shall I stay?"

Delia knew her half sister was offering moral support and although Delia really could have used it she couldn't accept it. For whatever reason fate had arranged this that she'd never thought would happen, she was going to have to face it—and Andrew—on her own.

"No, it's okay. Go on home to Henry. I'll see you tomorrow," Delia told her, forcing herself to appear more confident than she felt.

"You're sure?"

"I'm sure. It'll be okay."

Marta looked from Delia to Andrew and back again, then she leaned in to whisper to Delia, "I'm so sorry."

"It's okay," Delia repeated.

Jack Hanson, Gwen and Marta left then and Andrew motioned to the restaurant's bar. "How about in there? It looks quiet."

Delia nodded and, for the third time, said weakly, "Okay."

Andrew ushered her to a small round table in a dimly lit corner of the bar. As he seated her, he said, "I know, no sour-apple martinis. So what will it be? Coffee? Tea? Milk?"

Delia nearly flinched at the mention of the sour-apple martinis that had gotten her into trouble in Tahiti. "Coffee is fine. Decaf."

Andrew called the order to the waitress who had begun to approach them and then sat across from Delia.

Not too far across, though. The table was very small and the chairs were positioned so that when Andrew took the other one his knees were only inches from touching Delia's.

It was something she was more aware of than she wanted to be. Just as she was suddenly more aware of how fantastic he looked in an impeccably tailored charcoal suit, and matching dove-gray shirt and tie.

And all she could think was that she was glad it was too early for her to be showing or to have put on weight anywhere but in her breasts. Breasts that somehow seemed to be jutting forward a bit more now...

"You look great," Andrew said after a moment of studying her, as well. "I still can't believe I'm here with you. I've thought about you more than I want to admit. Tahiti wasn't the same after you left."

His handsome face erupted into a smile that was a little lopsided to let her know he was joking. Or at least that he was joking to the extent that not much could diminish how incredible Tahiti was whether she was there or not. But the mention of the island offered Delia a way to delay the inevitable and she seized it.

"Your brother said you just got back from vacation today. Does that mean you were in Tahiti three months ago and took another trip now?"

The quirk of Andrew's lopsided smile increased. "No, I was in Tahiti all along."

"Really?" Delia said, unable to keep the surprise out

of her voice. "Hanson Media Group must have a liberal vacation benefit."

That made the smile waver and dim somewhat. "To be honest, today is my first day working for the company."

The waitress brought their coffees then, and when she'd left, Andrew said, "But we don't want to talk about that. I've had enough of business for one day. I want to talk about you. And what you've been doing since Tahiti."

There was a quizzical note to his voice, as if he were wondering about a secret romance she might have had.

"I've just been working since Tahiti," she said as if that should have gone without saying.

Andrew nodded but Delia had the impression that he was still on a fact-finding mission, even when he said, "I didn't get to congratulate you before. About the baby."

"Thank you?" she said, forming a question with her inflection because she wasn't sure how she was supposed to respond.

"So, when we were in Tahiti you told me you weren't involved with anyone and hadn't been in a long, long while," he said then. "Were you fudging the truth? Or considering yourself technically free because you were on vacation?"

He was definitely testing her.

"I wasn't fudging anything," Delia said. "I wasn't involved with anyone and hadn't been."

"Then you must have met someone as soon as you got back?"

"Excuse me?"

"The baby—it's due in six months, if my math is right, that makes you three months pregnant."

Delia stared at him, searching those traffic-stopping features for some sign of what was going on with him.

She'd been certain that Marta's comment had spilled the beans. So either Andrew *hadn't* put two and two together, or he was playing some kind of cat-and-mouse game. Was he feeling her out in hopes that he would learn that someone else *was* the father?

As she studied him it struck her that Jack Hanson had referred to Andrew as his *younger* brother. And since Jack Hanson seemed to be about Delia's age, she began to wonder just how old Andrew was. If he was young enough to be that naive.

"Are you all right?" he asked when she'd let silence lapse for too long.

"I'm not sure," she said under her breath, taking another, closer assessment of his appearance.

There were a few lines just beginning at the corners of his eyes, but since he'd told her in Tahiti that he took every opportunity to get to a beach, maybe those lines were more an indication of sun exposure than of age. Especially since he lacked the creases an older man might have around his mouth.

Of course he had the confidence and bearing of a man her own age, but if he was from the media-rich Hanson family and was well-traveled, social status and world experience could account for that.

Actually, the longer she sat there trying to figure out his age, the more she realized that she couldn't and before she was even aware she was going to do it, she heard herself ask, "How old are you?"

"Twenty-eight," he answered without a qualm, but obviously with some confusion of his own at the question that had come instead of an answer to his inquiries about the father of her baby. "How old are you?" he asked then, as if turnabout was fair play.

"Thirty-seven," Delia whispered, stunned yet again tonight as she began to consider the fact that not only had she allowed herself to be seduced by a stranger on a vacation, but by a stranger who was so much her junior.

"Thirty-seven?" Andrew repeated. "You? I've known twenty-year-olds who look older than you do."

"I'm thirty-seven," she said once more. "And you're *twenty-eight*...."

Andrew laughed slightly, still clearly unsure what was going on. "And that means what to you?"

"It means you're nine years younger than I am," she mused.

"So you can do math, too?"

"Better than you," she whispered again.

His well-shaped brows pulled together in a puzzled frown. "You really aren't all right, are you?"

"No," she confessed. "Only not the way you think."

But Delia began to wonder if she had an opportunity here that she'd believed she no longer had when Marta had revealed that she was pregnant. If Andrew was even half thinking that he might *not* be the father of her baby she had the opportunity to keep him in the dark about his paternity.

It wouldn't require much. She could merely say that yes, she had met someone when she'd returned from Tahiti. Andrew would never know the difference. He'd go through his entire life without a thought that her baby was his, too. And she could go on with her own plans, the plans she'd had until tonight when she'd so coincidentally encountered him again—she could have and raise her baby on her own.

Without a father to complicate it...

That came from the back of her mind. In the voice of her mother. And it jarred Delia.

Fathers are just complications, her mother had decreed numerous times. *We don't need them. We do just fine without them.*

Except that the McCrays hadn't always done so fine without them.

Maybe it wasn't wise to make her decision at that moment, influenced by childhood hurts and before she'd considered all the angles, but on impulse Delia said, "I haven't lost my mind and I also didn't meet anyone— or even date anyone—since coming back from Tahiti."

The frown on Andrew's face deepened. "And you weren't involved with anyone *before* Tahiti...?"

"No."

Delia could see that his mental wheels were beginning to turn faster because he sobered considerably.

"Artificial insemination?" he asked.

She wasn't sure whether or not she was imagining a note of hope in that question, but the mere chance that it was there made her feel bad. It made her almost sorry she'd chosen this course after all.

But now that she'd planted the seed, she knew it was going to sprout one way or another and so she said, "No, not artificial insemination."

Andrew stared at her but there wasn't appreciation or happiness to see her or anything good in his expression now. Now he looked as if someone had caught him off guard with a sharp blow to the solar plexus.

He didn't speak. And Delia could tell that he was unable to bring himself to ask that final, inevitable question.

But she answered it anyway.

"Andrew, the baby is yours."

She saw him swallow hard enough to make his Adam's apple rise above his shirt collar.

"This day can't be real," he muttered to himself.

Delia thought that could only mean that he'd had a particularly bad day that this news had topped off. But bad day or not, it was hardly a heartening reaction.

She sat up straighter, drew her shoulders back and, fully intending to tell him she expected nothing from him, she said, "It's okay—"

"Not by a long shot," he said, cutting her off and standing abruptly.

His dark eyes bored down into hers as he shook his head in denial. "I can't do this right now. I'm sorry. I…I don't even know what I'm supposed to say. Or do. I…I guess I have to think," he rambled.

And then he turned around and walked out.

Out of the bar.

Out of the restaurant.

Chapter Four

Tuesday was a bleak, rainy June day in Chicago. An unusually chilly wind gusted from the west. It was the kind of day that could drag down the energy level of a native Californian all by itself.

But Delia's energy level didn't need help from the weather to be reduced. Although she hadn't suffered any morning sickness, she was more tired than was normal for her. A good night's rest was a must. And she hadn't had it. In fact, she'd had almost no sleep Monday night. Not after Andrew's hasty departure from the restaurant had left her stressed out.

She'd still been awake and checking the clock until almost 4:00 a.m. Then she'd dozed off but for only a couple of hours before she'd awakened with a jolt.

From a dream in which she'd been chasing Andrew down a deserted street, unable to catch him or to make him stop when she called to him.

It had been a ridiculous dream, she told herself as she drove to the Meals Like Mom's kitchens where she spent the lion's share of every Tuesday making sure quality control was being upheld and dealing with any problems at that end of the business.

A completely ridiculous dream. Chasing Andrew? The subconscious was a strange thing to come up with something that absurd. After all, she hadn't even had any intentions of tracking Andrew down, let alone of chasing him or trying to catch him. For any reason.

Yes, at one point when she'd first learned she was pregnant she'd contemplated contacting someone at the resort in Tahiti and seeing if she could at least garner Andrew's last name. But she'd gone through a whole lot of contemplations since learning she was pregnant. Different contemplations for each of several stages she'd experienced.

The first stage, she supposed, had been when she hadn't had her period two weeks after arriving home from Tahiti. She hadn't even entertained the idea that she might be pregnant then, though. Her cycles often varied and it wasn't unheard of for her to miss one, so she'd written it off to travel and stress and time changes, assuming that in a week or two she'd simply get back on course.

Then her second period had failed to appear. And she'd suddenly discovered herself in a state of alarm. Oddly enough, not alarm that she might be pregnant, however. Her initial fear had been that something else entirely was going on. She'd been terrified that she'd contracted some sort of sexually transmitted disease that had come from doing something as irresponsible as having unprotected sex with a stranger.

Punishment. She'd been afraid she was being punished for the one rash act she'd ever allowed herself.

So she'd taken her embarrassment to the doctor, confessed, and asked to be tested for STDs.

It had been the doctor's suggestion to also do a pregnancy test.

Even though it was difficult for Delia to believe it now, the chance that she might have gotten pregnant in Tahiti hadn't occurred to her, and the doctor's insistence that a test be done for that, too, had been the first occasion on which Delia had begun to think about that possibility.

Pregnant?

She hadn't *felt* pregnant. Not that she had any idea what being pregnant felt like. But she'd felt just like herself and it had seemed as if pregnancy would make her feel different somehow.

Of course she had been a little tired, but as a result of that she'd also been sleeping better than ever.

And she'd also been a little more hungry than usual, but she'd been working hard to make up for the time she'd taken off for Tahiti.

Her breasts had been more tender—attributable, she was sure, to the built-up hormones of the missed cycle.

But pregnant? She still hadn't accepted that as a genuine, honest to goodness likelihood.

Except that it had not only been likely. It had been the reality.

No, the doctor had assured her two days after her initial appointment when she'd returned to the clinic, she did not have any STDs. She was as healthy as a horse.

She was just pregnant. According to the blood test, which the doctor had insisted—when Delia had questioned the results—was conclusive.

Delia had taken the rest of that day and the next one off work.

She'd gone home, closed her drapes, changed into her pajama pants, an old sweatshirt and her fluffy tiger slippers, and collapsed onto the couch.

She hadn't turned on her television or stereo. She hadn't eaten. For a day and a half she'd done almost nothing but stare into space.

And think, *I'm pregnant?*

It had seemed inconceivable.

Inconceivable that she'd conceived.

A baby.

In Tahiti.

With some guy she didn't know…

That had been the second stage—total shock. And even worse, shame. And mortification.

She was thirty-seven years old, for crying out loud. And there she was, an unwed mother. No different than a teenager. No different than her own mother…

But somewhere in beating herself up had come stage three—the realization that *she* had come from her own mother's transgressions. That so had Marta and Kyle.

That they were good and valuable human beings who contributed to the world. That they were all grateful to be alive and to have each other. And that Delia's own baby could be just as good and valuable and grateful to be alive…

Father or no father.

And that was when she'd entered stage four—she'd begun to come to grips with the souvenir she'd brought back with her from Tahiti. She'd reminded herself that she was a capable, successful single woman who owned two branches of Meals Like Mom's, who made enough money to support a child on her own. That she *was* thirty-seven and that her childbearing years could be fast approaching extinction. That this might be her only opportunity to have a child at all.

Stage five had begun then. Stage five, where she'd come to feel that this baby was a stroke of fate, one that had given her this child as a gift. A gift she was happy to accept.

At about that point she'd toyed with the idea of calling the resort for Andrew's last name. She'd wondered if she should—or could—locate him somehow. If she should tell him about the baby.

But what if she actually *did* find him and tell him? she'd asked herself.

Andrew had only been an indiscretion she'd had on a trip far away from home. The same thing she'd been for him—one wild night on a tropical beach. After a whole lot of sour-apple martinis. That was the extent of it. What could she realistically expect to come of something like that?

Nothing, she'd ultimately realized. And there wasn't anything she'd *wanted* to come of it. It wasn't as if they'd had a relationship. They hadn't even exchanged last names or places of birth or job descriptions or family histories. They hadn't gotten to know each other in any way. Well, in any way but physically. And just the once. But that was nothing to build on. There was nowhere to go from that. No reason to pretend that something of substance had existed between them or ever might.

And as for the feelings of Andrew and the baby…?

Yes, she'd considered that, too.

But given her own family history, Delia doubted that Andrew would welcome the news that unplanned fatherhood had resulted from their single night together. Instead she'd decided that it was far more probable that her pregnancy would be information Andrew would rather not have.

And the baby? Well, Delia would make sure the baby did just fine. If anyone knew how to deal with a fatherless child and everything that child would think and feel, it was her.

So that had been that.

She'd gone from denial to disbelief to actually wanting this baby and being excited that she was going to have it. On her own. Alone. She'd accepted that. Embraced it. And stayed her own course accordingly.

Only now fate had added another twist. Now she'd met up with Andrew again.

And if that wasn't complication enough, she'd also learned that he was only twenty-eight.

"Nine, count them, *nine* years younger than I am," Delia said out loud. "Maybe being attracted to boy toys is a genetic thing."

In Tahiti it hadn't seemed as if there were any age difference between them. If she had had any inclination whatsoever that there was, she wouldn't have spent ten minutes with Andrew. Marta and Kyle wouldn't have *let* her spend ten minutes with him since they felt the same way she did about older women with younger men. And with good reason.

But there honestly hadn't been any evidence of an age difference between Delia and Andrew. In fact, looking back and analyzing it, she was convinced that Andrew's travels and the knowledge he'd gained from that, coupled with his take-charge attitude, had made him appear decidedly older than Kyle, who was also twenty-eight.

But no matter how Andrew had appeared or seemed, the fact remained that he *was* twenty-eight. *Only* twenty-eight.

"The father of my baby is a baby himself," Delia muttered as she arrived at the Meals Like Mom's kitchens and parked in her spot.

She turned off the engine but she didn't get out of her car. She just sat there, staring at the building's brick wall in front of her, thinking, *Andrew is not only a baby, but a baby who completely freaked out and ran away last night....*

Which didn't make him appear or seem older than he was anymore.

So she had probably been right to conclude that her

pregnancy was something he would rather not have ever known about, she told herself.

But it was too late now. He knew.

He knew and he wasn't still in Tahiti or some other place that allowed distance to aid this whole situation. He knew and he was in Chicago. He *lived* in Chicago. They might even be working together....

No. *That,* at least, she had some say in, she thought to console herself when everything felt as if it were careening out of control. They *didn't* need to work together. She could take her advertising somewhere else.

It wasn't much consolation, though. Not when she was still faced with the other two wrenches that had just been thrown into the works.

Andrew did know about the baby.

And he did live in the same city she did.

But there was nothing she could do about those two things.

There was nothing she could do about anything but her own situation. Nothing she could control except her own actions.

And when it came to that, there was comfort in realizing that nothing else had changed.

It didn't alter her own plans in any way. She would still have her baby and would support and raise it on her own.

And if seeing Andrew again the previous evening had served to remind her how pleasant he could be? How good he was at putting everyone around him at ease? How smart and charming and personable he was?

Well, it was nice to know that her child would have the potential for some positive genes that went beyond Andrew's staggering looks.

And it didn't make the slightest difference to her that one glance at him had made her heart skip a beat.

She was sure that that had purely been a result of the shock of seeing him. Not due to the fact that he was knock-'em-dead gorgeous.

And even sexier than she recalled, too…

"That's it for now. You can all get back to work. Except Andrew. You and I need to talk."

His brother's edict only vaguely registered with Andrew. Of course most of what had been discussed during the meeting that he'd spent the last hour in had gone right over his head, too. He couldn't concentrate. Or do much else. He hadn't slept. He hadn't eaten. He'd barely managed to get to the office in one piece since he'd been distracted by his own thoughts on the drive from his apartment, too. The truth was, in the short course of twenty-four hours so much had happened that he just plain didn't know which end was up.

"Andrew! Where the hell are you today?"

Jack. Right. Jack.

Andrew glanced around the conference room where everything had begun the day before, where this morning's meeting had just been held. Everyone else was gone. The door was closed. Only he and Jack were there. But Andrew had no recollection of the other attendees leaving.

Jack was sitting at the head of the table. Andrew was midway down one side, stiffly attempting to keep from slumping and giving in completely to the weight of all that seemed to have been dumped on his shoulders since yesterday.

"Sorry," he said to his older brother, even though he wasn't quite sure what he was apologizing for. But Jack's tone was impatient so he knew something was wrong.

"Well?"

"Well what?" Andrew asked.

"Well, I just asked you what went on with Delia McCray after I left you alone with her last night. But seeing as how you missed it, I'm back to wondering what the hell is wrong with you. You spent the whole meeting staring into space, unfocused, not responding even when something was addressed to you, acting as if you weren't really here, and now you still can't answer a direct question. What's going on?"

Andrew shook his head and stared at the tabletop, unsure if he should be frank with his brother or not.

"What does that mean—shaking your head?" Jack said, his voice rising a decibel.

Andrew shrugged. "I guess it means I don't know. I don't know what's going on with me. I got in from Tahiti yesterday and apparently when I thought I was opening my suitcase I was really opening Pandora's box instead."

Andrew forced himself to look at his brother in time to see Jack frown fiercely at him and shake his own head. "What does that mean? You opened Pandora's box because you have to work for a living now? Please. The last thing I need is more drama."

"I'm not being dramatic," Andrew said, a tinge of anger peeking its head through his stupor.

"Can we get down to business?" Jack said then.

"Isn't that what I'm here for?"

"We haven't established that you're actually here at all. But if you can pretend to be, for just a minute, maybe you can tell me about the McCrays."

"I met them in Tahiti. There's a brother, too. Kyle."

"And did you all hit it off?"

Andrew shrugged again. "They're nice people. I overheard them talking about snorkeling and offered to show them the best spot for it. Then I spent the next day with them, doing that." He omitted the fact that he'd also spent the evening with them. And the night with Delia. Which had, through the course of the last half day, become something he didn't want to think about.

"Do they like you?" Jack asked, as if the right answer might be tantamount to striking gold.

"I don't know," Andrew responded, his own tone somewhat ominous.

"They were friendly towards you. In a reserved sort of way. And then Delia McCray stayed to have coffee with you."

That was a leading statement. But Andrew didn't let it lead anywhere but to a confirmation. "Right."

"So what happened? Did you close the deal? Persuade her to give Hanson Media Group the top spot on the list of possibilities? What?"

"We didn't talk business."

"How could you not talk business? That's why we were there. Discovering a connection to the client, using it as a springboard, that's a plus when it comes to sales. And you didn't even bring up the subject after I left?"

Jack's anger was growing.

"We had other things to talk about."

"Nothing as important as Delia McCray giving us her advertising," Jack said, raising his voice again.

"Something more important," Andrew said under his breath.

"There isn't *anything* more important right now."

Andrew closed his eyes against the burn of sleeplessness, clasped his hands together, propped his elbows on the conference table and dropped his brow to his thumbs.

"I'm afraid there is," he muttered.

Jack hit the table and even though Andrew couldn't see him, he knew his brother had gotten to his feet. "Dammit, Andrew, what are you talking about? What did you do, fool around with Delia McCray in Tahiti and blow this for us before we even got a chance?"

"Maybe," Andrew said quietly.

"*Maybe?* Maybe what? Maybe you fooled around with Delia McCray in Tahiti or maybe you blew her account for us?"

Jack was shouting now. Andrew knew his brother was under a lot of pressure, but so was he.

He opened his eyes, raised his head from his hands and stared daggers at Jack. "There's no maybe about my *fooling around* with Delia in Tahiti. That baby she's going to have? Mine."

Jack stared back at him and for a moment there was a certain amount of satisfaction for Andrew in seeing that, for a change, he'd dished out the shock rather than been the recipient of it.

But it was only a moment before he realized what he'd just done. He'd just told his brother that he'd fathered Delia McCray's baby. Something he was a very long way from coming to grips with himself yet. Let alone being in any condition to face whatever his brother's response was going to be.

"Tell me that's a joke. A bad joke, but a joke," Jack ordered in a voice that was suddenly so quiet it was much, much more dangerous than any loud rant.

Still, Andrew had reached his own limit and he met Jack's glare eye to eye. "It isn't a joke."

"Sweet holy mother of—" Jack said as he threw his hands in the air and turned away, presenting only his back to Andrew.

But it was enough to let Andrew know that Jack was too mad to even look at him, to trust himself to say or do anything until he gained some control.

Andrew merely waited. What else was he going to do? Pandora's box really was open and there was no closing the lid now.

A full five minutes passed before Jack faced him again. Two fists went to the top of the conference table and Jack leaned on them and let his eyes bore into Andrew.

"Do you have any idea what you've done? Hanson Media Group is still reeling from the porn scandal. The meeting you just zoned out of was about how many more advertisers have pulled their accounts from us. They're leaving us in droves. Our competitors are cashing in on it, luring our clients away. Even clients who have been with us from the get-go are bailing. The wolves are at the door and you just unlocked it."

"Oh, come on. My personal business has nothing to do with Hanson Media Group," Andrew insisted.

"You may think this is just your own personal business, but it isn't," Jack said, his voice rising again. "Word of this leaking out—and things like this always do leak out somehow—could be the last straw. It could be what does us all in. David and I are breaking our necks trying to convince the whole damn world that Hanson Media Group would never be involved in por-nography in any way, shape or form. That we're a fam-ily-owned and -operated company with a commitment to values—family and otherwise. That we're respon-sible and upstanding and as wholesome as apple pie. And now you think it's only your own personal busi-ness that you had a sleazy one-night stand—"

"It wasn't sleazy. Delia isn't that kind of woman."

"Okay, a non-sleazy one-night stand with a poten-tial client. And you think it's your own personal busi-ness that you were too damn stupid and irresponsible to use a condom, and that now that woman—who you are not married to—is *pregnant?* You don't think that reflects back on the family? On the business? That it doesn't give ammunition to every single person who's rooting for us to go under and using morality as leverage against us?"

"Now you have to be joking," Andrew said, holding

on to his own temper, but by only a thread. "This isn't the Victorian era, Jack. People sleep with each other. Yes, sometimes they even have one-night stands. And even though they know better, sometimes they even have unprotected sex. We're human. Even the Hansons."

"We can't afford to be *human* right now!" Jack yelled. "We have to be better than that to prove ourselves all over again."

"Obviously it's too late for me to prove I'm better than anyone," Andrew shouted back, losing his tenuous hold on his own mounting anger. "So what do you want me to do?"

"Fix it! Take responsibility for your actions! Wake up to the fact that you're an adult and start behaving like one! For the first time in your worthless life, surprise me—surprise us all—and be a man!"

"And a *man* would do what?" Andrew asked, his teeth clenched now.

"Marry her!" Jack commanded.

"Marry her?" Andrew repeated in disbelief.

But that was when he saw something in his brother's expression that he'd never seen before. Something intolerable.

He saw disgust.

He heard disgust in Jack's voice when Jack said, "That probably would be too much to expect from you, wouldn't it? Doing the right thing for once?"

Then Jack pushed himself away from the table and stood ramrod-straight, towering above Andrew. "Everything David and I and everyone else around here have done since Dad died, everything I've given up, could all be shot to hell because of you. More people could lose their jobs. This family could lose what's kept it going for three generations. Because of you. I can't even look at you right now," Jack said, spinning on his heels and storming out of the conference room.

Because of you....

Because of you....

His brother's condemnation seemed to echo off the walls as Andrew once again found himself deserted in that particular office space.

He let his head fall to the back of his chair as wave after wave of emotions washed over him. Fury and anger. Insult. Frustration. Confusion. Bewilderment. Resentment. Fear and worry. And complete and utter dismay.

Marriage? Andrew thought. Jack actually wanted him to *marry* Delia? A woman he didn't even know?

Jack couldn't be serious.

But Andrew knew he had been.

In his brother's eyes it was either marriage or risk the entire fate of Hanson Media Group, of the family finances and of the livelihood of numerous other people employed by the company.

"Because of me."

Andrew took a deep breath and exhaled slowly.

Never in his life had the urge to run been so strong. The urge to simply get on the next plane out of Chicago and head for some tropical isle. The urge to leave behind all the complications, all the emotions, all the burdens, all the recriminations.

Only this time Andrew knew he couldn't do that. And not just because if he did, the money he needed to live wouldn't be forthcoming anymore. Also because it would support what his brother had just said about him—that he was irresponsible. That he was a child.

A stupid, irresponsible child.

Nice. Nice to know that that's what his brother and his uncle and the rest of his family thought of him.

Okay, yes, he'd lived a privileged life, thanks to Hanson money. And yes, that privilege had allowed him few responsibilities. And no, he hadn't done what Jack had done—become super-achiever in spite of all Hanson Media Group had provided. But he *was* a grown man. And just because he didn't have a lot of responsibilities—or hadn't had until yesterday—didn't mean he was *ir*responsible.

But the fact that that's what his brother and his family thought of him…? It was like wearing a hair shirt. It felt bad. Really bad.

But would it honestly take *marrying* Delia McCray to show Jack and anyone else who thought of him like that that they were wrong?

Drastic. That seemed too drastic.

Except, of course, that proving his naysayers wrong wasn't the *only* reason to marry her. She was, after all, pregnant.

Another ripple washed over him. This one something that closely resembled panic. The same kind of claustrophobic panic he'd experienced the previous day when he'd had to accept working here.

But a job was one thing. Marrying someone he

didn't even know was something else entirely. Being a husband—a *father*—was something else entirely…

He swallowed with some difficulty and closed his eyes for the second time, pinching them tight against the sting.

And there in his mind was the picture of Delia.

Odd, but in all of this, he hadn't thought much about her. He'd thought about her being pregnant. About the baby being his. Now he was thinking about what his family thought about him. He was worrying about what kind of an impact his next action could have on people who were just nameless faces outside of his office. But Delia? Sweet, sunny Delia—who had been on his mind a lot since he'd hooked up with her in Tahiti—had not been what he was thinking about since last night.

And odder still, seeing her in his head, thinking about her, suddenly made him feel better. Not a lot, but some.

Yet the idea of *marrying* her continued to just be bizarre.

Marriage?

Him?

To Delia?

No, even just trying the idea on for size didn't help. It still seemed totally surreal.

But was it the only way to redeem himself in the eyes of his family? The only way to *do the right thing*.

The right thing—Jack's words.

They seemed old-fashioned. Archaic, even. Or maybe he'd been out playing around for so long that his concept of what was right and what was wrong had progressed too far. Far enough to become skewed. So skewed that the notion of marrying the mother of his child seemed weird to him.

The mother of his child—now *that* seemed weird. But that's what Delia was now. And that's what he had to deal with. The consequences of his actions.

Consequences that reached far beyond what they would have been had he *not* been a Hanson. Had he not been in the middle of this Hanson Media Group mess.

But he *was* a Hanson. And he was in the middle of the Hanson Media Group mess. And maybe this was where he finally paid the piper. Where he paid for the luxury and privilege he'd enjoyed so freely.

"So, for the greater good and to prove myself, I have to marry Delia?"

Have to…

Another old-fashioned idea. And not a particularly appealing one.

But Delia herself was appealing, he thought. In Tahiti and last night, too.

And as for the baby?

Okay, the thought of becoming a father was daunting. Especially when he considered that he didn't have any idea what kind of father he would make. When he considered that he hadn't had the greatest role model in his own father.

But dealing with *that* wasn't going to happen right away, he reminded himself to keep some sense of control. First things first. And first he'd deal with the hurdles that had been shoved in front of him and get over them, and then he'd have some time to adjust to the other…

So, *was* he actually considering the whole "do the right thing" marriage? he asked himself, slightly surprised that that seemed to be where he was ending up.

Yeah, maybe he was coming to that, he thought. Maybe there really wasn't any other choice. Not if he ever wanted his family to think of him as more than a screwup. Not if he didn't want to spend the rest of his life as the person who just might have struck the final blow to Hanson Media Group's existence. And not if he didn't want to be the kind of guy who got someone pregnant and then turned his back on her.

Which all boiled down to one thing.

Marriage.

To Delia.

"It'll be all right," he said forcefully to reassure himself.

But despite his outward show of bravado, despite his conviction that he wasn't the stupid, irresponsible kid his brother had accused him of being, despite his sudden discovery that he just might want to do the right thing, at that moment, faced with making a living and marriage and fatherhood, he felt pretty unprepared for it all.

Hell, he felt completely unprepared for it all….

Chapter Five

It was after nine o'clock that night when Delia left her office at Meals Like Mom's headquarters. After spending the day at the kitchens she'd had to return to the main office to do some paperwork. Because everyone but the cleaning crew had been gone by the time she'd arrived—and even the cleaning crew was gone now—she was alone when she left the building.

She wasn't the only person in the parking lot, however. When she got there, there was a second car parked in the spot next to hers—a Jaguar sports coupe—and a man was getting out from behind the steering wheel.

Had she not recognized him instantly she might have been uneasy with the situation. But she did recognize him so she continued the short walk from the building to her car.

"Andrew?"

"Hi," he said, closing his car door without taking his eyes off Delia.

He didn't look good. Well, he was good-looking enough never to look bad—especially in a navy blue suit that rode his broad shoulders and narrow hips to perfection. But it crossed Delia's mind that he must have slept even less than she had because he looked exhausted and drained, and his handsome face was as strained and stressed as any face she'd ever seen.

"Are you okay?" she asked as she came to stand at the front of her own sedan.

"Sure," he said, sounding as if he were putting too much effort into being chipper. "How about you?"

"I'm fine," Delia answered, but with a query in her own tone to let him know she didn't believe he was all right. "What are you doing here?" she asked then, not beating around the bush.

He held up a file folder. "I have the formal proposal based on what we discussed over dinner last night. I thought I'd get it to you as soon as I finished it. And maybe we could talk."

"It's late and I've done about as much work as I'm going to do today. I'll take the proposal and look at it tomorrow." And go home and try to figure out why she was feeling disappointed that that was the only reason he was there.

"It isn't business I want to talk about," he informed her quietly. Then, with a nod at the coffee bar across the street he added, "How 'bout I buy you a cup of decaf? I promise to stick around long enough to drink it tonight."

The half smile he flashed her way was deadly. Even if it did have shades of shame and embarrassment to it. In fact, that made it all the more appealing, somehow.

But Delia reminded herself of all she'd hashed through since the evening before. She reminded herself of their age difference. And of how nothing could ever come of anything between them. Then she said, "I don't think so. I think it's better if we just go our separate ways and pretend we never met."

"I don't think we can do that," he said, his natural charm in the cock of his head.

"Sure we can. Had we not met again purely by coincidence that's what would have happened, so let's just let it happen anyway."

"You never even thought about trying to find me? To tell me about the baby?"

"I considered it. But it didn't seem realistic that I'd be able to find you. And even if I had... Well, I just decided not to."

He nodded slowly, his dark brown gaze on her the entire time.

Delia thought he might be willing to accept what she was proposing, that he would figure that it was enough that he'd come back, made contact, given her the opportunity to take this further if she wanted to. And that since she was making it clear that she didn't want to, he'd feel let off the hook and this would be the end of it.

Which should have made her happy.

But somehow the sense that he was going to do that depressed her a little.

He surprised her though. "I don't want to go our separate ways and pretend we never met," he told her. "I can't do that. I don't think I would have wanted to do that even if there wasn't a baby and we'd met again, but now that there *is* a baby, it really isn't an option."

There was more strength and certainty in his voice than she expected there to be. He wasn't wavering. And not only wasn't he accepting the out she was giving him, he was letting her know he wasn't allowing her to brush him off, either.

"Come on," he said then. "A cup of coffee. Right across the street. So we can talk. That's not a big deal."

"It's late…." Delia said, still hedging, almost afraid to have coffee with him when she could feel herself succumbing to his appeal all over again. Even against her will.

"It isn't late. It's not even nine-thirty," he said insistently. "One cup of coffee. If you're too tired to walk over, I'll drive."

The coffee shop was close enough to make that suggestion funny and Delia couldn't help smiling. She also couldn't help giving in, despite knowing without a doubt that she shouldn't.

"One cup of coffee," she said, warning him with her tone that that was the extent of what she was willing to concede to. "And I don't need to be driven across the street. Even if I am nine years older than you are."

He grinned and leaned toward her as if to share a confidence. "That wasn't an age-related remark."

But there were a lot of other age-related issues that Delia made a mental note to keep in mind as they headed across the street.

When they got to the coffee shop Andrew seated her at a corner table and then went to the counter to get their beverages. As Delia sat there waiting, she felt compelled to watch him. Actually, she couldn't take her eyes off him.

He really was a striking man. Even with signs of fatigue and stress tightening his features. Tall and straight-backed, he emanated power and strength and confidence. More than she would expect of a man not even thirty yet.

The white shirt he wore under his suitcoat was minus the tie she assumed he'd had on all day, and the collar button was unfastened, exposing a thick neck she suddenly remembered—all too well—kissing. Hot and solid, that's the memory she had. With smooth, smooth skin...

"Here we go," he said as he returned to their table carrying two cups of coffee.

Delia yanked herself out of her reverie and silently chastised herself for the direction her thoughts had wandered. Recalling anything about being with Andrew in Tahiti was forbidden—she'd decided that this morning—and she was sticking to it.

"Thank you," she said, glad the place was so dimly lit, because she was concerned that her very fair skin might have some kind of telltale blush to it to go with those thoughts that were off-limits to her.

Andrew sat in the chair across from her and crossed

one calf over the thigh of his other leg, grasping the calf with his right hand.

For no reason Delia understood, her gaze went to that hand, relishing the sight of long, thick fingers, and again flashing back to the taboo of Tahiti—to that hand on her breasts, those fingers…

Again she put effort into altering the course of her thoughts and forced her eyes and her attention back to Andrew's face.

"So," she said to encourage him to say whatever it was he'd wanted to talk about over coffee, hoping to keep herself in line that way since she was failing miserably otherwise.

"So," he repeated, his eyebrows arching in what appeared to be lingering amazement. Tinged with perplexity. "A baby."

"A baby," she parroted him this time.

"Wow."

Delia just nodded.

"Are you…healthy?"

"Very."

"Do you have, I don't know, morning sickness or anything?"

"I've actually felt fine."

Andrew nodded this time, and Delia noticed that he had a death grip on his coffee cup as he raised it to his mouth and took a drink. And if she weren't mistaken, he had some trouble swallowing as she sipped her decaf and watched him over the rim of her own mug.

Then he said, "What about…emotionally? Are you all right with…a baby?"

"I really am," she assured without hesitation. "I admit when I first found out I was kind of knocked for a loop—"

"Right," he said, as if there were finally something they had in common.

"But after a while I realized that I'm okay with it. Better than okay, I'm happy about it."

He nodded once more but Delia could tell it was difficult for him to identify with the concept of being happy about this situation. So she qualified it.

"I'm older, remember? And my 'having baby' days are numbered. So for me, after I adjusted to the idea, I decided maybe it was a good thing. Not something I'd planned, or something I would have gone out and purposely done, but since it happened anyway, I'm okay with it."

Andrew nodded yet again but it was obvious he still didn't share her sentiments. "Well, that seems like a good way to look at it."

He did more tight-fisted coffee drinking. Then he looked her in the eye and said, "I don't doubt the baby is mine. I know we should have used something that night and we didn't and that's my fault. And the timing maps out, and... Well, I'm sure you didn't look up at me unexpectedly last night and instantly figure there's somebody to pin it on."

Delia's expression must have shown her negative reaction to what he was saying because he put both big hands up, palms outward, as if to stop something, and said, "I'm sorry. That sounded bad and I didn't mean for it to. I'm just... I've had a lot of shocks and changes in the last two days. And no sleep. I'm not firing on all burners. I'm just trying to say that I know that you aren't the kind of person who would say the baby was mine if it wasn't."

"Actually, you don't know what kind of person I am. But no, that isn't something I would do. I have no reason to."

"And since I'm not questioning that it's mine, I want to do what I'm morally obligated to do. I want to marry you."

Delia laughed. Not because what he'd said had been humorous, but out of reflex because it was so absolutely ludicrous. "Excuse me?"

"I want to marry you," he said again and Delia had the mental image of someone holding a gun to his back.

"Because you want to do what you're morally obligated to do," she repeated his words.

"Right."

"Just the kind of proposal every woman longs for," she said sarcastically.

"And the answer is…"

"No," she responded as if it were ridiculous to expect any other answer. "Not on your life. Not in a million years. Never. No way. Not a chance."

"Did you want to take a minute to think it over?" he deadpanned with a half smile.

"You really do need sleep. And maybe a psychiatrist if you're seriously suggesting we get married," Delia told him. "Why on earth would we do that?"

"It *is* something people do. Particularly people who are going to have a baby."

"Maybe in some cases, but you and I? We don't even know each other. And I don't need to be made an honest woman of. I'm not going to be shunned or thrown out of the tribe or ostracized or stoned or branded or something. This isn't the Dark Ages. I don't need or want anything from you. Marta is already onboard as my birth coach. Kyle and Janine will come out for the occasion, and between them and Marta and Henry, I'll have plenty of help for as long as I need it after the baby is here. And from then on, I had every intention of doing this myself before last night. Nothing has changed because you and I just happened to meet up again. Certainly you don't have any *moral obligations* or any other kind of *obligations* to me."

"Okay, I've made you mad. I'm sorry. I know I'm not doing this right."

"You don't need to *do* this at all. I'm sure you mean well, but the truth is, having and raising one baby on my own is better than raising two babies at once—the one I deliver in six months and the one who fathered it—"

Delia hadn't meant that to sound quite as harsh as it had, and the fact that her words made Andrew draw back, as if he'd been struck, stalled them.

He inclined his head and breathed a wry sort of sigh. "Two hits on good old Andrew in one day. First from my brother and now from you. Somebody must have declared it open season on me and not sounded the alert."

Delia didn't know what he was talking about but she took a few deep breaths to calm herself before she said,

"I'm sorry. That was uncalled for. All I'm trying to say, is that you can relax. You're not on the hook here. You wouldn't have been if we hadn't accidentally crossed paths again and there's no reason that should change now—"

"What if I want it to change?"

In spite of what he said, Delia didn't have the sense that there was much conviction behind it.

"You're young, Andrew. Younger than I had any idea you were in Tahiti. I can see that you aren't ready for this, while I, on the other hand, am. I'm ready financially, emotionally and in every other way there is. I'm ready to have this baby, to raise it, to love it and cherish it and be thrilled that I've been given it. So there's no reason for you to do what you *aren't* ready for."

Delia stood then, wanting to show him through her actions as well as what she was telling him, that he genuinely was off the hook. "Forget we ever met in Tahiti or again here. Forget my name. Forget I even live in Chicago. Go on with your life and I'll go on with mine, and we'll both be better for it."

She walked to the door of the coffee shop then and had to pause for two couples to enter.

By the time she got outside, Andrew was there behind her.

"What if I don't want to forget you and everything else? What if I think that we're having a baby together and we should do it together? What if I want to be a part of that?"

Delia barely glanced up at him as she headed back

across the street to the Meals Like Mom's parking lot. "What if *I* think this is just some kind of grand gesture that's coming out of a misguided notion that it's what you're supposed to do when the truth is, you don't want to be a father at all?" she countered.

"The *truth* is, you don't know what the truth is because you don't know me any better than I know you. So you can't know whether or not I'm ready for this or might be dying to be a father."

Delia couldn't suppress a small smile at that. "I know enough to know you aren't dying to be a father," she said with full confidence.

They'd reached their cars by then and Andrew insinuated himself between her and the driver's side door, requiring her to look up at his face. "You don't know any more about me than I know about you," he said again. "You can't. And maybe that's really where we need to start."

"We don't *need* to start anything, anywhere," Delia insisted.

"We've already started a whole new human being," he pointed out with a glance downward at her midsection that, for no reason Delia understood, sent a little thrill through her.

Then he continued. "If you won't agree to marry me now, then at least agree to give me a chance. Say you'll spend some time with me, that you'll let us get to know each other, that you'll think about going from here."

From here to nowhere, Delia thought.

It seemed obvious to her that what she'd said in the coffee shop had provoked him. That he'd taken it as some kind of challenge. A throwing down of the gauntlet. A gauntlet that he was now determined to pick up. Probably because he *was* so young. But she felt certain that any course set only to meet some imagined challenge to his manhood would be short-lived.

Still, if agreeing to see him was what it would take for him to give up the ghost on this, then it occurred to her that maybe that's what she should do. That maybe if they did get to know each other some, they could even reach a more realistic approach to whatever role Andrew might decide he wanted to have in the baby's life in the future. And that maybe that would be better for all three of them.

"All right," she conceded with a weary sigh.

"All right, on second consideration you *will* marry me? Or all right, you'll spend some time with me, getting to know me?"

"*Some* time," she qualified.

"And you'll do it with an open mind," he said as if he'd been reading hers and knew she was only humoring him because she didn't honestly believe anything substantial would come of it.

"With an open mind," she repeated.

He smiled down at her. "That's all I need," he said with another show of that confidence and charm that had been so appealing in him from the start.

Unable to contain it, Delia returned his smile. "Can I go home now? It's been a long day."

He nodded but his dark eyes held her there in spite

of it as if he were seeing her for the first time. And enjoying the sight.

Then, in a tone of voice that was very like what had gotten her out onto the beach with him that night in Tahiti, he said, "You know, I had no idea you were any older than I am. I even thought I had a year or two on you. So if we're going to forget anything, let's forget the age thing, huh?"

"I doubt I'll be able to do that," Delia confessed.

"Try," he urged in little more than a sexy whisper.

Then he leaned forward only slightly.

It may have been nothing but an alteration of posture. But still it flashed through Delia's head that he was going to kiss her. And she got out of the line of fire in a hurry.

"But we aren't in Tahiti anymore and now everything is different. Now we're in the real world," she warned in a way that could have been only referring to the difference in their ages, or could also have let him know there would be no kissing—or anything else— if that's what had been on his agenda.

But if kissing *had* been on his agenda he gave no indication of it and again said, "Try," as if they were still only addressing the age issue.

Then he slid away from her door so she could unlock it.

He opened it for her when she had, holding it as she got in.

Which she did. Fast.

Because suddenly she couldn't stop recalling kisses

she'd allowed from him before the one she thought she might have just shunned. Kisses she'd participated in.

And how great they'd been…

"I'll be in touch," he promised.

For the second time Delia merely nodded, half wondering if he actually would be in touch.

And half imagining him really touching her.

Really kissing her.

And really doing more to her.

More that she had to struggle to keep from fantasizing about the entire drive home.

Chapter Six

"I am so, so, so, so sorry!"

Delia hadn't been in her office on Wednesday morning long enough to put her purse in her desk drawer when Marta came in, closed the door and fell back against it to relay her apology. It was the sixth one since Monday night when her slip of the tongue about the wine had revealed Delia's pregnancy to Andrew, his brother and the advertising executive at their dinner meeting.

The first apology had been in a message from Marta on Delia's answering machine by the time she'd arrived home Monday night. But it had been too late for Delia to return the call without waking Henry, so she'd refrained.

Tuesdays were always busy days for both Delia and Marta. Delia spent her time at the kitchens, while Marta was also away from the office at the transportation center to deal with matters there. They almost never had contact with each other on a Tuesday. This week Marta had called five times—with more contrite messages—throughout the day and evening. But Delia's cell phone battery had been dead and when she'd finally collected all the messages and called Marta back, Marta had been away from her own phone so Delia could only leave her a message.

Apparently Marta had made sure to get in early enough this morning to be watching for Delia, though, so they could finally connect.

"I know you said in your message that you aren't furious with me, but are you sure you don't want to just kill me?" Marta continued before Delia had the chance to respond. "I wouldn't blame you if you did. Or if you wanted to disown me or fire me or never see me again as long as you live."

With a laugh, Delia put her purse away, sat in the leather chair behind her desk and finally said, "I'm not furious with you and I don't want to do any of those other things, either. You know better than that."

Marta pushed away from the door and crossed to the visitor's chairs, wilting into one of them. "I couldn't believe it when the words came out of my mouth. Of all the stupid things to do—mention the pregnancy with Andrew there. And *Andrew!* Did you have any idea at all that he *would* be there?"

"How would I have had any idea? I didn't even know

Jack Hanson's brother's name was Andrew, let alone that he was the Andrew from Tahiti," Delia answered.

"Did you just about pass out when you saw him?"

"Just about."

"Me, too. What are the odds?"

"It was pretty amazing," Delia agreed.

"But still, shocked or not shocked, I should never—*ever*—have opened my big mouth about the baby in front of him."

"Actually, he didn't put two and two together. I ended up telling him myself. So you didn't really do any damage. I could have said just about anything and he would never have questioned it."

Marta's face showed her disbelief. "It didn't occur to him that the baby was his?"

Delia shook her head. "No. I thought he had figured it out, too, but he hadn't. He didn't have even an inkling that it's his."

"Seriously?"

"Seriously."

Marta rolled her eyes. "Men. They can be so dumb sometimes."

"Especially the really young ones," Delia said somewhat under her breath because she wasn't eager to get into that part of the story despite the fact that she knew there was no avoiding it.

Marta looked appropriately confused. "The really young ones?"

"How old did you think Andrew was when we were in Tahiti?" Delia asked.

"About your age, I guess. I didn't really think about

it. You two looked so good together and he fit in so well—"

"I thought he was about my age, too," Delia said. "But when he seemed kind of naive about the baby stuff Monday night I asked how old he is."

"And?" Marta urged when Delia dragged her feet about revealing what she knew would be as big a sticking point with Marta as it was with her.

"He's twenty-eight," Delia said with a grimace.

"*Twenty-eight? Kyle's age?* No."

"Yes. Twenty-eight. *Nine* years younger than I am."

Marta sobered considerably and Delia read into it.

"I know. Boy toy. Deep down I must be as bad as Peaches."

"You aren't like our mother," Marta said forcefully. "Andrew didn't seem at all a boy toy, and that was always part of the appeal for her, if you'll recall. They were always incredibly immature and very obviously a gazillion years younger. That isn't true of Andrew."

"I don't know…" Delia hedged.

"Andrew isn't obviously young and immature. I thought he was older than Kyle and you know what an old soul Kyle is," Marta insisted.

"When I told Andrew on Monday night that the baby is his he ran like a rabbit—right out of the restaurant. Just like when Peaches told Kyle's father about Kyle when he was three—remember?"

"I remember. He was in such a rush to get out of there that he knocked over my bicycle."

"Well, if there had been a bicycle in his way Monday night, Andrew would have knocked it over, too. I thought that was the last I'd ever see or hear from him again. Just like Kyle's father."

"But you've already seen or heard from Andrew again?" Marta guessed.

"He was in the parking lot when I left here last night. He wanted to talk, but he looked like he was facing a firing squad."

"Still, he came back and wanted to talk," Marta said, surprising Delia by defending Andrew. "What did he have to say for himself?"

Delia told her, omitting nothing. Including Andrew's marriage proposal.

Marta's eyes widened when she heard that. "What did you say?"

"What did I say?" Delia repeated as if she couldn't believe the question that had been asked reasonably. "I said no, of course."

Marta didn't respond to that except to raise her eyebrows.

"What? You think I should have said yes?" Delia demanded as if that were the most absurd idea yet.

Marta shrugged. "I just don't know that I find the idea of you marrying the father of your baby as outrageous as you seem to."

"It's too early in the morning for jokes, Marta."

"I'm not joking."

"You have to be. This is a twenty-eight-year-old guy I don't even know."

"Right. Who also happens to be your baby's *father*."

Delia deflated slightly in her chair, resting her head on the back of it to stare at her half sister.

"I'm just thinking," Marta continued, "about how much you and Kyle and I craved having a dad around when we were growing up. And what if your baby is a boy? Since we're reminiscing, remember the first jock-strap fiasco when Peaches took Kyle to buy one?"

"She made him try it on over his jeans in the aisle of the store," Delia recalled.

"Right. And after that poor Kyle did everything he could to find a male influence. He was on the list of every mentoring program he ever heard about. He was always beating the bushes for someone to toss a foot-ball with him or take him to a baseball game."

Delia was beginning to feel less certain of the position she'd taken with Andrew.

But even if it showed it didn't keep Marta from going on anyway.

"And what about you?" Marta persisted. "That's how we ended up in Chicago in the first place. It's why you live in the house you live in. Maybe you should think about whether or not you really do want to turn up your nose so easily at the opportunity to give your baby what none of us had—a live-in dad married to its mom."

Delia hadn't thought about it like that. She'd just rejected Andrew's proposal out of hand because it had seemed so utterly insane to her. Putting it in the terms Marta had just put it in, though, gave her pause.

Still, there were other things—important things— that were unchanged.

"But he's only twenty-eight, Marta," Delia said.

"And proposal or no proposal, I don't think he has the kind of staying power or tenacity that Kyle has. He's… I don't know, I just had a really strong feeling that he was proposing because he thought he had to, that he was going through the motions, not that he was doing anything he honestly wanted to do."

"So you said no without considering it."

"Yes."

"And did he breathe a sigh of relief and say he was glad you hadn't taken him up on the offer?"

"No."

"What did he do?"

"He said we should get to know each other," Delia admitted, thinking for the first time that Andrew's persistence said something positive about him in spite of his age—and she was giving him credit only now that her sister had pointed out that he *hadn't* breathed a sigh of relief because she'd turned him down.

"Getting to know each other seems reasonable," Marta remarked. "And like a mature way to proceed."

"I don't know how mature it was. It was just… It was just like an excuse not to end everything right there and then. Which was what I was trying to do."

"But you didn't succeed," Marta guessed.

"He wouldn't have it. I ended up agreeing to see him again, to spend some time with him and get to know him, but I still had—and have—my doubts about whether or not I'll hear from him again."

"And if you do?"

"I guess I'll have to stick to my word and see him. Get to know him."

"Give him a chance," Marta said as if finishing what Delia had been saying.

"Give him a chance at what?"

"Maybe making things work out between you? For the baby's sake?"

Delia shook her head, having difficulty believing what she was hearing from her sister. "There isn't anything between us *to* work out. And *for the baby's sake?* Are you actually suggesting that I try to have a relationship with and maybe *marry* someone just for the sake of the baby?"

Marta shrugged. "I'm just thinking, Dealie," she said, using the nickname Marta and Kyle had had for her since they were all kids, "that you liked Andrew well enough to sleep with him in Tahiti. There must have been *something* there or you wouldn't have done that, because that is *sooo* not you. And even if you don't end up marrying the guy, maybe you should at least try to be on friendly enough terms with him that he can be *some* kind of a dad to the baby—if nothing else, an 'occasional phone call' kind of a dad, or an 'exchange cards now and then' kind of dad. But just a dad the baby can know is out there in the world for him or her, if he or she needs him."

Delia gave her half sister a sympathetic smile. "Is there a little of your own childhood wish fulfillment in this, too, maybe?" she asked gently.

"Okay, yeah," Marta admitted. "I wasted a lot of time calling my father, trying to get him to visit, trying to get him to say I could turn to him if I needed to. But that's the point, hon. Kyle did the mentoring thing, I begged for acknowledgment and a safety net, and you came all the way to Chicago—what it boils down to is that every one of us went to extremes to put a father or a father figure into our lives somehow. Just in case your baby wants to know his or her father, wants him in his or her life, maybe you should give Andrew a shot. And who knows? He could surprise you."

Delia was glad to get home Wednesday evening at the end of another long day. Another long day of work and worry, and of the added strain of half hoping that every phone call her secretary informed her of, every opening of her office door, might bring Andrew into the picture again. That he might actually make good on his claim that they should get to know each other.

Not that it was for her sake, she made sure to tell herself a hundred times throughout the day. But after having talked to her sister, it did seem as if maybe, for her baby's sake—as Marta had said—she should keep the lines of communication open with Andrew.

And if she'd felt disappointed each time the call was *not* from Andrew? That was for her baby's sake, too, she told herself. Only for her baby's sake. Not because deep down she might have been hoping to hear Andrew's voice on the other end of the line.

And if she'd felt the same kind of disappointment each time there had been a knock on her office door and it had opened to reveal her secretary or Marta or someone else she worked with…? That had definitely been for the sake of her baby and not because she was hoping to glance up and see the carved features of

Andrew's remarkable face or that honed body that managed to inspire far too many memories for her.

It was only the baby she had in mind. The baby and the baby's future. A future that Delia was beginning to think would be fatherless after all, when her doorbell rang.

She was upstairs in the circa-1945 house she'd inherited from her grandmother five years before. She'd just changed out of her dress clothes into a pair of jeans and a gray hoodie T-shirt. Zipping the hoodie up, she descended the steps that ended in a small entryway only a few feet from the heavy walnut door.

When she looked through the peephole, she discovered that face she'd been hoping to see all day long. Distorted by the wide-angle lens and barely lit by only the illumination of her porch light, but that unmistakable face nonetheless.

Andrew.

And there she was in her laying-around-watching-television clothes, with her hair caught up in a rubber band at her crown just to get it out of her face.

Still, if she ran back upstairs to put on something better and redo her hair without answering the door, Andrew would think she wasn't home and leave. So, wishing she looked a whole lot more fabulous than she did, she opened the heavy wooden panel to him.

He smiled and raised both arms from his sides, showing her multiple bags with various fast-food logos emblazoned on them.

"Burgers, fries, tacos, burritos, chicken sandwiches,

salads, chili, hot dogs and fried chicken—can we have dinner?"

Delia had to laugh. "For about two weeks. If you want to die young," she answered, bypassing any greeting, too.

"Or we could order pizza," he added.

"Feeling gluttonous?"

"No, I just want to find something that will get me in the door."

"Then you should have brought donuts and cookies," Delia confided guiltily.

He grinned and looked over his shoulder at his car parked at the curb. "I can go back if that's what it will take."

In spite of having allowed herself to be convinced that continuing contact with Andrew might be what she should foster for the baby's sake, and despite all her disappointments during the day when it hadn't been him on the phone or at her office door, Delia still didn't think she should feel quite as elated as she did to have him standing on her front porch. Because seeing him again pleased her so much she actually felt giddy, and that didn't seem like what she should be allowing to happen.

So she tried to temper it by taking a deep breath, reminding herself that he'd run scared on Monday night and that on Tuesday night he had appeared looking as if he'd been through the wars in coming to the decision to see her again. And although none of that haggard appearance was there tonight, she didn't think she should lose sight of the difficulty he'd clearly had in making himself set this course.

"Okay, I'll give you a minute to think it over," he said when she let too much time lapse while her mind raced.

Still, Delia didn't rush to invite him in. Instead she took a closer look at him, searching for lingering signs of reluctance. But the haggard appearance was definitely gone tonight. He was wearing slacks, a T-shirt and a short, lightweight leather jacket that added to the effect and seemed just right against the still blustery June weather.

"Come on, what do you say?" he cajoled when she really had left him standing there longer than she should have. "Can I tempt you with junk food or do I need to go in search of donuts and cookies to sweeten the deal? Because I'll do it, if that's what it takes. Even though you *did* agree to spend some time with me and this is some time…."

The way he looked hadn't aided the cause of toning down her giddiness, or her pleasure in seeing him again but she finally stepped aside anyway and said, "I do need to eat," as if that were the only reason she would let him in.

He stepped across the threshold, out of the way of the door so she could close it. Once she had, Delia turned back to him, finding him standing in the center of her entryway.

Against the aged and scarred dark wood paneling that was on nearly every downstairs wall outside the kitchen, it struck her that Andrew was like a diamond in the rough in her modest, dated house.

He glanced around—into the living room to the

right, up the stairs, down the hallway that led to the kitchen in the rear—and said, "This is not what I expected of someone who owns two branches of a very successful business."

"No?"

"Not that it isn't an interesting old place with possibilities for improvement," he amended. "But—"

"I know, it needs a whole lot of remodeling and refurbishment. But I inherited it as is, and I've needed to devote all my time and energy since then to getting Meals Like Mom's going in Chicago in order to stay here. So I haven't been able to do anything. The remodel is in the works, though. I've hired a contractor and a decorator, and we're getting started by the end of the month so everything will be redone by the time the baby is born."

Andrew again held the bags aloft. "Why don't we eat while this stuff is hot and then you can give me the tour and tell me what you're planning?"

That seemed innocuous enough. "Okay. There isn't a dining room—that's one of the additions I'll make. So that leaves us either eating at the kitchen table or the coffee table in the living room. Your choice."

From the distance of the entryway, Andrew eyed the oval-shaped coffee table in front of her white sofa. "Doesn't look like that's big enough for all this stuff. We'd better do the kitchen."

"Good choice," Delia said, adding, "It's back here," and leading the way to the family-sized space that sported a beautiful round pedestal table surrounded by cane-backed chairs.

The table and chairs were the only nice things among the cupboards that were painted to match the walls and appliances so out-of-date Delia was surprised they still worked.

"It's Incredible Hulk green," Andrew commented as he followed her into the space lit poorly by a single fixture in the center of a high ceiling.

"I know, it's awful. The kitchen will have to be gutted. Everything's going—cupboards, appliances, the chipped and speckled linoleum, and the color, for sure."

"The table and chairs are nice," Andrew said as Delia took him there and he set the sacks of food down.

"The furniture is all mine."

"Then you *do* have taste. That's a relief," he joked.

"You doubted me?"

"Not until I saw this place," he said with a laugh.

He took off his leather jacket then and for no reason Delia understood, she couldn't tear her eyes away while he did. Why such a thing should intrigue her seemed completely irrational, but there she was, drinking in the sight of those broad shoulders spreading like an eagle's wings. That strong, powerful chest thrusting out to stretch the confines of his T-shirt. And something inside her went weak.

So weak she actually felt the need to pull out a chair and sit down.

Although when she did, that put an entirely different portion of his anatomy into her line of view. And looking at his zipper brought a whole other element to mind.

"Sit," she said a bit urgently as he hung his coat over the back of the chair across from her.

He finally did as she'd commanded and Delia forced her gaze to his face. His oh-so-handsome face…

"Tell me again what all we have here," she said, turning her focus to the safety of the food to prevent herself from any further ogling.

"A little of everything," he answered, naming each item as he peered into one bag after another.

"So what'll it be?" he asked when he'd listed everything once more.

"I'm a sucker for the Mexican food. I'll go with a burrito. And maybe a little salad. But I don't know what you're going to do with the rest of this stuff."

"My roommate will eat anything."

"You have a roommate?" Delia asked as Andrew took one of the burgers for himself and set the French fries between them so she could have a few of those, too.

"Mike Monroe," Andrew answered. "We've been friends since we were kids. It was sort of an upstairs-downstairs kind of a thing, I guess you'd say. His mother was the nanny for a family that lived near where I grew up. Part of her work arrangement was that she keep Mike with her while she was with the family's kids and that Mike be sent to the same schools. His mom thought she was getting a better education for him and letting him hobnob with kids who could end up being business contacts or names to know when he got out into the world. The trouble was, everyone knew he was the nanny's kid and they just gave him a hard time."

"Everyone except you?" Delia asked as they both ate.

Andrew shrugged. "Trust fund aside, I had more in common with Mike than with anyone else and couldn't have cared less who his mother was. Actually, I thought he was just lucky not to have a stepmother, the way I did."

That last comment was fraught with disdain but before exploring it, Delia said, "And the two of you— you and Mike—still live together?"

"Mike disappointed his mother by not becoming some big-deal businessman or something. He's a writer. A good one, but still he's doing the starving artist thing. So we share my place. Hanson Media Group pays the rent and all the utilities and insurances and whatnot—which means Mike doesn't need to contribute anything to that—and his being there gives me someone to take care of whatever comes up when I'm traveling. It works out for us both."

Delia imagined a fraternity house, but she didn't say anything about that. Instead she addressed something else she was wondering about.

"So was Hanson Media Group paying for everything even before Monday?" she asked.

"Yes," Andrew responded, as if he didn't quite get the question.

"It's just that you said Monday was your first day on the job," she explained.

"Right," he confirmed after washing down a bite of

burger with one of the sodas he'd brought. "But before Monday Hanson Media Group—or at least the Hanson fortunes—paid for everything without my working for the company."

"Did you work somewhere else?"

"Nope. Not a day in my life," he said, clearly having no clue how that unsettled her.

Then she recalled something else he'd said. "Last night you mentioned a lot of shocks and changes—I'm assuming the baby is one of the shocks…"

"That's an understatement."

"But it seemed as if there were other shocks and changes, too," Delia said in a quest to learn what was going on with him. "Was one of the others that you needed to go to work?"

"That was definitely another shock and change. I was told on Monday that if I want to keep the money coming in, keep the apartment and the rest of the perks I've enjoyed, I now have to work for the family business—hence my new job as advertising salesman. That was a *substantial* shock and change."

"How do you feel about that?"

He grinned at her. "Doesn't seem like as much fun as snorkeling in Tahiti."

In other words, he wasn't enthusiastic about the idea. Any more enthusiastic than he was about the idea of the baby.

"You *have* had some shocks and changes," Delia remarked.

He merely smiled at that, giving no clue as to what

else he might be thinking or feeling in regards to the severely altered course he'd encountered.

He *had* given some indication of his feelings about his stepmother, though, and so it was that that Delia returned to.

"You said something about thinking Mike was lucky that he had a real mother rather than a stepmother. Were your parents divorced?"

"My father was widowed. My mother died when I was fifteen and the next thing we knew—"

"We?"

"My brothers and I. Besides Jack, there's my brother Evan, the middle son," Andrew explained. "The next thing we knew, my father had gone out and married Helen. Without any fanfare, he just sprung her on us one day, announced that they'd gotten married. He was fifty-eight, she was thirty-one. His trophy wife."

"And she was an evil stepmother?" Delia guessed.

"No, she wasn't evil. She certainly tried with us. But…I don't know, we just never liked her. We resented her. She was… Well, she was his trophy. He dressed her, jeweled her, gave her elaborate gifts to make sure everyone knew how successful he was, but when it came to Helen, Jack, Evan and me? We just never connected."

"Not even now? As adults?"

"'Fraid not. I can't speak for anyone but myself, but I hated that my mother had just died and here was this other woman as some kind of replacement part plugged into the slot. Even if that worked for my father, it didn't work for me. So right out of the gate I didn't like the *idea* of Helen. From there, no matter what she did, I just didn't have it in me to play son to her. I pretty much dismissed her as a nonentity. She was nothing more to me than someone who coexisted in my house. And as soon as I could get out of that house—or what I felt was left of our home after my mother's death— I got out and away from Helen. I went to college."

He said that as if there were something amusing about it.

"So you *did* go to college?" Delia said to urge him to explain himself.

"Two years' worth. Not enough to get a degree even if I *had* passed everything. But the truth is, I spent more time partying than studying, so I barely got by before I dropped out. I was hardly what you'd call a serious student. But at least by then I was old enough to be on my own, to get the apartment. Which kept me far away from Helen, and that was what I wanted."

"Do you speak to her or see her now at all?"

"Unfortunately. I'm civil to her, but that's about it. I definitely don't have any soft family feelings for her. But then I don't think we Hansons are really what anyone would consider a particularly close family— not the way yours is. It isn't as if you'd ever find the four of us vacationing together in Tahiti," he said with a wry chuckle.

"Not even you and your brothers?"

"We go our separate ways. In fact, old Jack is beating his head against a brick wall right now trying to get Evan to come back and help out with Hanson Media Group, too, and apparently isn't having much luck.

And he and my uncle—David—are both up in arms about it."

"So not even your father's death has brought you all closer?" Delia asked.

"It's brought me back to Chicago and in close proximity, and it will probably eventually bring Evan back, too, but beyond the fact that we'll all be here again? I don't know that we'll end up the way you seem to be with Kyle and Marta."

"That's sad," Delia said.

Andrew merely shrugged as if it didn't affect him that way.

Delia had all she wanted to eat and apparently he had, too, because he pushed away the wrapper he'd been using as a plate and said, "So why don't you show me around this dungeon and tell me what you have planned for it?"

Delia assumed the question was a hint that he wanted to change the subject.

Since she thought that it might be better if they did before she learned more about him that made him seem young and at a very unstable time of his life, she said, "Okay."

She gathered all their used wrappers, containers and plastic utensils into the empty sacks and took them to the trash under the kitchen sink. Along the way, she said, "That was the first thing I thought about the house, too—that all the dreary paneling down here makes it seem dungeonish. But wait till you see the orange bathroom upstairs and the candy-cane pink bedroom. They'll make you wish there was paneling hiding it."

"Was the person who lived here before color-blind?" he asked with a laugh.

"I don't think so, but to tell you the truth, I don't know," Delia said. "I don't know anything about her."

Turning back to the table, Delia realized that there was still a lot of food left in the remaining bags there.

"We'd better put the rest of this stuff in the fridge until you go home or your friend will end up with food poisoning," she suggested.

"I'll do it," Andrew volunteered, taking it all to the short, chubby refrigerator.

He dwarfed the antiquated appliance and Delia was again struck by both the glory of the big, strapping man and how ill-suited he was to these surroundings.

And to her, too, she thought, telling herself that that was something she needed to keep in mind.

But all she was really thinking about at that moment was that the evening wasn't ending yet.

And that she was unreasonably happy about that fact.

Chapter Seven

Once the leftovers were stored, Delia led Andrew out of the kitchen and began the tour, first of the downstairs and then of the second level where there were four bedrooms and a single—orange—bathroom.

"It's easier downstairs to add on along with using the mudroom in back to expand the kitchen and add the dining room, family room and half bath. But up here it would be more complicated, so I'll combine the two smallest bedrooms into a master suite with its own bath and much better closet space than I have now."

Andrew poked his nose into the bathroom and then into the bright pink room. "Color-blind. I'm convinced," he joked.

"I'm using the pink room as my own now," Delia

continued. "The other two smallest rooms are what will be combined for the new master suite and bath. When that's finished, I'll move in there and the pink room's closet will be broken down to make it a decent-sized guest room that will also be connected to the main bath. The nursery will go in the original master bedroom, which is a fairly decent size already and only needs paint and carpeting to be ready to go. That makes it the easiest to redo, so I can be sure it's finished in case the addition and remodel takes longer than planned," she explained, feeling strange talking about the baby with him. So strange she wasn't even sure she should have.

"Quite a project," Andrew commented.

The fact that he hadn't responded in any way to her mention of the baby or the nursery made her wonder if he might rather she not mention the little souvenir she was carrying at all.

"It's a huge project," Delia agreed, trying to ignore his omission. "But at least the basic electrical wiring and the pipes are okay. If that had had to be redone, too, it would have been even worse."

Andrew moved to the guest room to glance into it, too, but he never went anywhere near the room that would be the nursery.

Delia had the feeling that he not only didn't want to see it, he wasn't even ready to acknowledge the need for it. And she thought that was something to take as seriously as she took their age difference.

"It should be nice when it's finished," he said then. "It's a great old house. Solid. Interesting."

"I think so, too," Delia said, fighting the sinking sensation in the pit of her stomach. Even as she told herself that Andrew's lack of interest in her nursery plans shouldn't matter.

She headed downstairs again with Andrew following behind.

"I can make coffee," she offered then, sounding more chipper than she felt.

"Not for me, thanks."

"Tea?"

"No, I'm fine," he said as they reached the entryway once more.

This is where he runs again, she thought. *Where the pregnancy and the baby have become real enough to scare him away.*

Well, fine, she told herself in her internal dialogue. *Go! And don't come back. Don't drag this game out any longer than necessary. Get out and leave me alone and let me do this the way I planned to do it before Monday night. It's better like that anyhow....*

She was so certain that running out was exactly what Andrew was going to do, that she actually headed for the front door to open it for him.

And then he surprised her once more.

Rather than running out on Delia the way she'd convinced herself Andrew would after she'd shown him her house and he'd shied away from every reference she'd made to the baby and the nursery, Andrew nodded toward the living room from the entryway and said, "How about if we sit in there?"

"Oh. Okay," Delia agreed, barely concealing her shock.

Then, correcting the few steps she'd taken toward her front door to let him out, she made a quick—and she hoped subtle—detour to go into the living room ahead of him.

She turned on the lamps on each of the end tables that bracketed the sofa as Andrew sat in the center of it and patted the spot beside him in invitation to her.

Delia didn't want to appear rude by going to the overstuffed chair positioned to one side of the couch, so she accepted the invitation. But not without getting as far away from him as she could, sitting with her back pressed tightly to the arm of the sofa and angling to face him with one leg upraised in front of her as a barricade. Just in case.

"Did you say you *inherited* this house?" he asked then, turning slightly in her direction so he could look at her and settling one long arm on the top of the sofa-back.

That brought his hand only a breath away from the knee over which she was peering at him. Close enough for her to see every well-tended nail, every knuckle, every inch of that hand that she suddenly recalled touching that same knee. Squeezing it before taking a slow slide up her thigh and around to the inside of it…

"Delia?"

She was still staring at his hand rather than answering him and he'd caught her at it. She altered her focus quickly and went just as quickly back through her memory, searching for what he'd asked her.

She was grateful when it came to her.

"I did say I inherited the house, yes," she confirmed, hoping he hadn't asked her anything else after that that she'd missed.

Apparently he hadn't because he went on naturally from there. "How did you inherit a house from someone you don't know or know anything about?"

"How do you—"

"You said it a little while ago, when I asked if the person who lived here before was color-blind. You told me you didn't know because you didn't know the person who lived here before."

Delia had forgotten.

"That's right," she mused, flattered that he'd been paying more attention than she had and appreciating the fact that he was trying to get to know her.

"So how did that come about?" he prompted when her thoughts distracted her from answering immediately once again.

"I inherited the house from my father's mother," she informed him.

"Your grandmother? And you didn't know her?"

"We never met. I didn't know she even existed. Until she didn't anymore and the attorney who was handling her estate tracked me down in California to tell me she'd left me the house."

"Was your father on the outs with his family?"

Delia wished a simple family feud was what she could tell him about, because even now it embarrassed her to reveal her background to anyone.

But in the interest of her own child, she swallowed

her embarrassment and plunged in. "I never met my father, either."

Andrew's eyebrows arched. "You never *met* your father?"

"I wasn't raised…conventionally. None of us were— not me or Marta or Kyle. Our mother—who we were never to call Mom—"

"What were you supposed to call her?"

"Her name—Peaches."

"Peaches? You're kidding?"

"No, that was her name, Peaches McCray. She was not what you'd call a traditional kind of mother. She was different. A lot different. A lot more…freewheeling, I suppose you could say."

"How could she be anything else when she'd been named Peaches?"

"Oh, she named herself Peaches. She was born Beatrice McCray on a farm in Kansas. But the day she turned eighteen she went to court and changed her name legally to Peaches—because that was her favorite food. Then she got on a bus and left town."

Delia could see that Andrew didn't know whether to laugh or sympathize because his expression was a combination of both humor and astonishment. And she'd only begun.

"Okay. Peaches," he said. "Go on. I'm still waiting for the part about how you never met your father and inherited this house from his mother."

"Right. Well, Peaches wanted to be a movie star. Not an actress, there was no studying of a craft or anything. She wanted to be a star—with a capital S and an exclamation point. So she took the bus to Holly-wood, where she was sure she would be discovered and never was. But she also never stopped thinking that it would happen and given that, it was important that she maintain the illusion of eternal youth."

"Are we talking past tense or present? Is she still living and wanting to be a movie star?"

"No, she died nine years ago in a jet-skiing accident. But what was true of her when I was a kid was true of her until the day she died."

"Did she look anything like you?" Andrew asked as if that would have been a good thing.

"Marta and Kyle think I'm the spitting image of her. For better or worse."

"For better," Andrew judged. "So appearing younger than she was must not have been too far out of her reach."

"No, it wasn't. But her own looks were not the only thing she used to keep up the illusion that she was per-petually twenty-five—"

"She also didn't let her kids call her Mom," Andrew said, proving he was listening now, too.

"Right again. Having kids—*three* kids—aged her, so we were introduced as the younger siblings she was raising after a tragic tornado had killed our parents."

"And her parents…"

"Were alive and well until not long ago. Living quietly on the farm in Kansas, not ever understanding what made their daughter tick."

Andrew's eyebrows arched even more. "Okay," he

said with an amazed sort of tilt to his head. "But we're still not up to the unmet-dad part."

"I'm getting there," Delia assured. "It *is* kind of a long story, though. Maybe you don't want—"

"No, I want to hear the whole thing."

"If you're sure."

"I am."

"All right then. Not only did Peaches use her looks and her story about Marta, Kyle and me as her siblings rather than her kids to keep up her eternal youth profile, she also absolutely refused to consort with men over a certain age. Your age, actually."

"Twenty-eight?"

"Twenty-eight was the crest of the hill, anything past that was over it for Peaches, and she preferred her male friends much younger. She was convinced that being with very young men made her seem like she was that young, too. And, to be honest, that was just where her taste in men ran. My own father was twenty-three when I was born. Peaches was thirty. Marta's father was barely twenty. Kyle's father was twenty-one."

Delia tried not to show her own discomfort with that fact. Or how ashamed she'd felt of her mother's affairs growing up. "Three kids by three different fathers and all without the benefit of a marriage or even a long-term relationship in the bunch. The fathers—like the other men who came before, between and after—were all just her boy toys...."

Delia stumbled over the term Peaches had reveled in. The term that had been used for Andrew this week, as well.

"I'm surprised Peaches had kids at all," he said.

"We were her accidents. That was actually how she referred to us. Affectionately, but as her three little accidents," Delia said, knowing it would never, ever be something she said to her own child. Not even affectionately. It had always stung anyway. And made her feel unwanted.

"Oh," Andrew responded as if he didn't know what else to say.

"I told you, Peaches was not a cookie-baking, storybook-reading, mother-earth kind of mom," Delia reminded.

"Did she not want to marry any of your fathers?"

"Absolutely not. Starlets—which was what she always considered herself, even as she got older and older—were not married. And none of our fathers wanted to marry her, either. They were young, most of them trying to be movie stars or actors, too. They were guys she met doing work as an extra on a movie or at one of her other odd jobs."

"How *did* she support three kids? I assume there wasn't a lot of child support paid by boy toys."

Delia didn't like that term any better when Andrew used it and felt a little ashamed of herself for referring to him as that when he said it with such disdain. "No, there was no child support. And we didn't live well, that's for sure. Peaches got all the work she could in the movies—being an extra in mob scenes was her biggest claim to fame. Otherwise she did whatever she could that was near to movie studios, hoping—"

"To be discovered."

"Exactly. She worked in a dry cleaners, waited tables, drove one of those buses that take tourists by the homes of famous people. She never kept one job for long because the minute she thought it interfered with something she believed would launch her into stardom—for instance, if her boss wouldn't let her off for a cattle call—she'd quit. Right there and then. Mainly we did a lot of living in studio apartments or trailer homes, and sneaking out in the middle of the night because we were months behind in the rent and didn't have the money to pay."

"How did you feel about living like that? About having a mother like that?" he asked, clearly trying not to sound judgmental. But Delia could tell he was passing judgment in spite of it. She understood that it was difficult not to.

"There were mixed feelings," she answered candidly. "I hated the uncertainty of it all. I hated having to move around and I definitely didn't like doing it like cat burglars. I really hated it the couple of times when we got caught and there were ugly scenes and the police were called on us...." Delia knew she wasn't helping the impression Andrew had so she cut that part short. "And of course there were always things that I wanted that we just couldn't afford. But I wasn't a miserable, unhappy kid, either. Some of Peaches's flamboyancy was fun. Nothing ever got her down—"

"Not even having the police called on her?"

"The few times that happened she'd managed to cajole the landlord out of pressing charges by the time the police actually got there, so everything worked out all right. And Kyle and Marta and I were closer than we might have been under other circumstances. I'm actually thankful for that because we have a great relationship. We've always looked out for each other, taken care of each other, known we could trust each other and depend on each other no matter what. I guess in a lot of ways, we found stability through that."

"So, are there parts of the way you were parented that you'll repeat?"

Delia laughed. "Don't sound so worried. I'm about as different from Peaches as it's possible to be, and beyond loving this baby unconditionally and being accepting of just about anything it is or does—which was true of Peaches—I have every intention of being as traditional a mom as I possibly can be."

Andrew seemed relieved to hear it. Relieved enough to return to what they'd been talking about before he inquired about her feelings about her mother. "So in all the time you were growing up there was never even a stepfather? Or one of the real dads who played a role in your lives?"

"Nope. Kyle's father didn't even know he existed until Kyle was three, and after Peaches told him about Kyle we never saw him again. Kyle doesn't have any clear memories of him but he did go to great lengths growing up to try to find a replacement." Delia grimaced slightly. "Marta's father showed up occasionally, but that was almost worse."

"Why?"

"He and Peaches sort of had an on-again, off-again thing. He was trying to act, too, so they'd meet up at different auditions. Plus whenever he moved, he'd let her know where he was, and she did the same whenever we moved. But he was… I don't know, he was *so* young when Marta was born and he wasn't the brightest bulb in the box, and he certainly wasn't a kid person. The rare times when he did appear he was awkward with Marta, standoffish. He just didn't seem to know how to relate to her and he definitely didn't give the impression that he wanted to. The trouble was, Marta wanted so desperately for him to love her, to be a dad to her, that as soon as she learned to dial a phone she started calling him, begging him to come see her or let her go to his place or take her somewhere. Begging him for some semblance of a father-daughter relationship that just never happened."

"Not ever? Even now?"

Delia shook her head. "Marta knows where he is and calls him once or twice a year to say hello and see how he's doing, but there's just no effort from the other end. He has nothing to say beyond that he's fine or getting work as a stand-in here and there. He doesn't show an interest in her or give her any indication that he feels a connection to her at all. When she and Henry got married she asked her father to walk her down the aisle—she even said she'd send him the plane ticket to come to Chicago so it wouldn't cost him anything. He said he was in a bind with his landlord and would rather she send him cash than a plane ticket."

"And did she?"

Delia nodded sadly. "I'm pretty sure she did. Kyle ended up walking her down the aisle, and her father didn't even call that day or send a card to congratulate her. She's just had to accept that he isn't ever going to be a father to her. Reluctantly, but there hasn't been any other choice."

"Which brings us to your father."

"Which brings us to my father," Delia conceded with a sigh.

"Who you never met."

"Well, I'm told that he showed up once when I was three days old, but I don't count that as my having met him."

"That was it?"

"That was it. He was from Chicago and I have no idea if he came back here after that or what. All I know is that he told his mother about me, about Peaches, that he died of hepatitis two years before his mother had a heart attack, and that since I was the only living relative left, his mother decided after his death to have a will made that gave me the house—the only thing she owned. She knew my name. My mother's name. And that we were last known to live in California. So when she died, her attorney got on the Internet and found me to notify me of the inheritance."

"That must have come as a surprise."

"It did. The attorney I spoke to had been hired by my grandmother after she found his name in the phone book so it wasn't as if he knew her or could tell me anything about her. She had just told him that her son— my father—had died and she didn't want the house to go to the state, so it should go to me."

"That doesn't inspire any warm fuzzies," Andrew said sympathetically.

"No, but at least she was letting me know that she knew about me and thought of me as some sort of family."

"And that was enough for you to leave California and your business there and move here?"

Delia smiled. "It wasn't that cut-and-dry. Marta and I came here to see the house, thinking that I would just list it with a realtor and sell it. But once we got here…" Delia took a deep breath and when she exhaled, it came out with a shrug and the need to fight a welling up of emotion that made her voice softer. "I don't know. Until that point I'd thought that I had dealt pretty well with the lack of a male parent in my life. Yes, there had been times when I'd wished for a dad. When I'd missed having one. But on the whole, I thought I'd adjusted better than Kyle and Marta had. That I had accepted things the way they were."

"And then you got here," Andrew said to invite her to confide in him what he seemed to realize wasn't easy for her to admit.

"Then I got here," she said. "And I guess the house felt like the closest thing I was going to have to a connection with my father or his mother, and I sort of wanted to absorb what I could of that."

Andrew took that hand she'd been so engrossed in earlier and used it to squeeze not her knee this time, but her arm where it was hugging her leg. A comforting squeeze that somehow managed to send little shivers of something sensual through her even as he succeeded at consoling her.

"The place gave you roots," he said.

Delia smiled and blinked back some moisture that had suddenly dampened her eyes. "Even if the roots were only peripherally mine," she joked. "I suppose a psychiatrist would have a field day with it. But for whatever reason, something about being here just felt like home to me. A tie to family, even if it wasn't much of a tie. Even if there wasn't a family anymore by the time I got here. Still, it was the best I could do, so I stayed and started the Chicago branch of Meals Like Mom's."

Andrew gave her a moment to gain some control of her emotions and then, just when she was wishing he'd say something else, he said, "And how did Marta come to stay with you?"

The fact that her sister had made her own home here had been a source of comfort and support for Delia, it was something she was grateful for, and so it made her smile again. "Henry was the realtor I was going to list the house with. Marta and Henry hit it off, so she stayed here, too."

"And that left Kyle to run the California end of the business?"

"It did. Which was good for him. It gave him more autonomy than he'd had before and he's really flourished with it. He's expanded operations and taken production farther than I probably would have if the status quo hadn't been disrupted."

"And you ended up with two branches of Meals Like Mom's."

Delia laughed. "Yes, but I've already gone on and on with the saga of my own background. I can't talk about the business stuff tonight, too."

"Okay, we'll save that for another time," Andrew said as if he were making a promise. "I do have one more question about the non-business end, though."

He took his hand away from her arm and Delia felt a wave of disappointment.

Still, she hid it and said, "Okay, one more question but then that's it for me tonight."

"Did you decide not to even try finding me to tell me about your pregnancy because of Peaches's track record with the fathers of her kids?"

"That was part of it," Delia answered honestly. "I've witnessed firsthand three examples of male response to unplanned pregnancy, and none of them led me to believe it would make a whole lot of difference if I did track you down and tell you."

"So you thought 'why bother'?"

"I'm afraid there was an element of that in the decision."

"But all three of you have gone to some great lengths to get even a semblance of a father in your lives. Seems like that might have factored into your decision, too."

"Except that the only one of the three of us to actually have the real thing around was Marta and that has been more negative than positive."

Andrew made a face. "That doesn't bode well for me."

Delia shrugged, not wanting to say that the ball was

in his court when it came to that, but thinking it just the same.

He read the shrug correctly. "Okay, so it's up to me to make it a positive or a negative. But now that I do know, and want to be involved," he added pointedly, "you don't have any objection, right?"

She still wasn't convinced that he really did want to be involved, wondering if he might simply be going through the motions. The way Marta's father had. But Delia didn't say that.

"Reservations, maybe. But no objections, no," she said with a tentativeness to her tone. "Although you should also know that if it turns into a negative—"

"It won't," he said with something that sounded as much like bravado as conviction.

Then he gave her a killer half smile so full of mischief it was infectious and said, "Or you could make sure it's a positive that I'm around by marrying me."

Delia laughed and teased him. "Who says that would make sure it was a positive?"

"It would be more a positive than if we aren't married, wouldn't it?" he challenged.

"Not necessarily."

"So what is that? Another no, you won't marry me?"

"Another no, I won't marry you," she said un-equivocally

"I guess I'll just have to keep trying, then," he countered, sounding undaunted.

Or maybe he was just able to sound that way because he was relieved that once again she'd rejected his proposal. Which Delia thought was more likely when she recalled his earlier reaction to her mention of the nursery and his total lack of interest in it.

He checked his wristwatch then and stood. "I took up your whole night. I'd better let you get to bed."

Delia didn't do anything to stop him. But she did discover another rise of disappointment in her. This time that she was losing his company the way she'd lost his touch before.

But again she concealed those feelings and stood, too.

"Don't forget the leftovers for your roommate," she reminded.

"I'll get them. My coat is in the kitchen, too," he said, heading in that direction.

Delia let him go, turning off the living room lamps while he was gone.

He had on the leather jacket again when he returned with the fast-food sacks in hand, and Delia led the way to the front door.

"Thanks for dinner," she said then.

"For what it was worth," he answered as she opened the door and he stepped near to the threshold.

He didn't go out, though. Instead he stopped there and turned to face her. "I had a good time," he said.

"I didn't bore you too much with the story of my life?"

"Not a boring life, not a boring story," he said as if he meant it.

There was honesty in his dark eyes, too, as they met hers and held them. Honesty and warmth and a huge helping of that appeal that had sucked her in so effectively in Tahiti. An appeal that kept her looking up at him and made something inside her soften.

He's only twenty-eight, she silently shouted to herself.

But at that moment it didn't actually register. At least not as anything important enough for her to break off that eye contact and send him home.

It didn't even register enough for her to rear back the way she knew she should have when he began to lean forward. Or when he got close enough for her to be sure he was going to kiss her. And kept on coming.

Then he did kiss her and even as she was wondering why she was letting him, she was kissing him back. She was savoring the feel of supple, talented lips parted over hers. Tantalizing hers with memories of that night in paradise while still providing an entirely new experience, since this was the only time he'd kissed her when her mind wasn't fogged with martinis.

And heaven help her, she liked it. She liked kissing him. She liked him kissing her. She liked it all more than she wished she did.

Enough so that she was sorry when it ended at just the right length for a first kiss that wasn't truly a first kiss at all.

When it had ended Andrew smiled down at her, his expression slightly dazed. "I remembered enjoying that. I just didn't remember how much," he said almost more to himself than to her.

Then he muttered a good-night and finally went out onto her porch.

Delia made herself close the door right then, when she was inclined to keep it open and watch him go all the way to his car.

But it was a minor gesture that didn't revoke the fact that she'd just let him kiss her. That she'd just kissed him.

And for some reason, even though she told herself forcefully that she shouldn't have done either of those things, self-loathing wasn't what she felt.

She felt all warm and soft and tingly.

She felt like she wanted him back there right then.

To do it all again…

Chapter Eight

"'Morning," Andrew said to announce his presence as he left his bedroom bright and early on Thursday and came across his roommate with a pretty brunette standing at the front door of the apartment he and Mike Monroe shared.

"Hey," Mike greeted in return, sounding as if he hadn't been awake long.

There was more evidence of that in the fact that Mike was wearing nothing but pajama bottoms. The woman around whose hips Mike's arms were draped, however, had on a running suit.

"Melanie, this is Andrew," Mike said then, performing a casual introduction. "Andrew, this is Melanie."

No last names. Andrew knew what that meant—Mike didn't know the woman by anything but Melanie.

"Good to meet you," Andrew said, moving on to the kitchen to leave them alone for what appeared to be a kiss he'd interrupted.

"You, too," Melanie called after him.

It was a variation of a scene that had played out innumerable times in the apartment, both for Andrew and for Mike. Bringing someone home to spend the night was hardly an unusual event. But for some reason, as Andrew went into the kitchen, this time it struck him as a stupid thing for them both to have done so capriciously.

Maybe because of where his last one-night stand had landed him.

He heard the apartment door open and close, and Mike wandered into the kitchen, too.

"New girl?" Andrew asked with an edge of censure to his voice that had never been there when he'd made the same inquiry in the past.

"I've been jogging again," Mike answered, giving no indication that he'd caught the tone. "I keep meeting Melanie on the path. We've talked a little. Joked around. Last night I finally invited her to come by for a post-run cooldown."

The pleased-with-himself smile Mike cast Andrew just prior to opening the big stainless steel refrigerator set off another wave of that same feeling Andrew had had only moments earlier.

Apparently it was reflected more in his expression than it had been in his voice, because when Mike turned around with the orange juice container and faced Andrew across the marble island counter, Mike finally took notice. "What? Do you know her or something?"

"No, I've never met Melanie before," Andrew said.

"So how come you look like that?"

"How do I look?" Andrew asked.

"Like you don't approve or something," Mike said, pouring two glasses of juice and sliding one to Andrew.

"A lot's happened with me since I got back from Tahiti," Andrew muttered darkly. "I guess I'm seeing things differently."

"A lot's happened, huh? Is that why I haven't seen you for more than five minutes? I wondered. Usually we've had our catch-up night out by now." Then, as if it had just registered with him, Mike added, "And what're you doing out of bed so early? Wearing a *suit*. Don't tell me there's been another death in the family."

"No, nobody else died," Andrew said. "But there's been plenty going on since my dad died."

Mike used his juice glass to point to the opulent living room just beyond the kitchen. "Let's take it in there, huh? I didn't get any sleep and I'm beat."

Andrew watched his friend walk to the other room and plop down on one of the leather and chrome chairs without a care in the world. And he envied him.

Maybe he envied him the night he'd just spent with Melanie, too. A night like so many Andrew had had himself—a night of fun and flirting and the excitement of being with someone he'd never been with before….

Andrew took his own glass and joined Mike, sitting

slightly slumped in the center of the cosmopolitan sofa that matched the chair.

Totally at ease, Mike put his bare feet on the glass coffee table and crossed them at the ankle. "So what's the story? Even if nobody else died, you look about as happy as if you *were* going to a funeral."

"Things are a mess," Andrew said, glancing from the big-screen TV in front of him to the wall of floor-to-ceiling windows that looked out over a park and made the apartment prime property.

It was strange, but seeing Mike with that woman had added an element to Andrew's feelings that he hadn't anticipated. No, he wasn't thrilled with the idea of a nine-to-five job selling advertising for Hanson Media Group, but seeing Delia again, spending a little time with her, had begun to make that portion of what he'd come home to slightly okay—only slightly—but slightly more palatable.

Now, though, seeing Mike, knowing Mike would go on the way they both always had, while Andrew might end up actually married with a kid, made that seem daunting again.

Could he really turn his back on this lifestyle? Tie himself to one woman? Raise a kid? Never have another night like the one Mike had just had?

"Geez, man, what's going on? This looks bad," Mike said with alarm when Andrew still hadn't explained anything.

Andrew glanced back at his friend and for the first time since he'd been home and everything had been dumped on him, he spelled it all out to someone.

By the time he'd finished, Mike didn't seem at all relaxed anymore. He'd taken his feet off the coffee table, placed them flat on the floor and was sitting hunched over, as if the full weight of Andrew's problems was bearing down on him, too.

"So now you're working *and* you're supposed to *marry* this woman? Just like that? Overnight?" Mike asked.

"That's what I've been told," Andrew confirmed.

"And your brother and your uncle are all over you to make you do both whether you like it or not?"

"No job equals no money, no apartment, no nothing. And if I don't get Delia to marry me… Hell, I don't even know what I'll be up against if I don't get *that* to happen. I thought Jack was going to pop a vein when he heard she was pregnant. He seems to think the whole future of Hanson Media Group is riding on my getting married and *doing the right thing. For once*—as he put it."

"But is that what you *want* to do?" Mike ventured.

"Get married? No, it isn't what I want to do," Andrew said, feeling a twinge of guilt over the fact that that was true, and that he was presenting the exact opposite impression to Delia. Delia, who he honestly did like. Whose company he enjoyed. Who he was still so attracted to that he'd imagined taking her into that upstairs bedroom of hers when she'd given him the tour of her house last night and seeing what it might be like to make love to her on a bed rather than on a beach….

But marriage? That was a whole different ballpark.

"Can't you reason with Jack?" Mike asked. "He can't think it's a good idea for you to be forced to marry somebody you don't even know."

"There's no reasoning with him. Or even with David at this point. They're doing everything they can to save the company and that's all they can think about. They need manpower, so I have to work. And they need the morality problems to go away, which they believe won't happen if I *don't* marry the woman I got pregnant."

"Man..." Mike breathed, shaking his head. "I'll bet you would never have had *that* one-nighter if you'd had any idea this could be the end result. I know I wouldn't have."

For no reason Andrew understood, he felt defensive of Delia.

"It isn't as if Delia isn't great," he said suddenly. "She is. She's gorgeous and fun to be with and smart. She owns her own business, she's ambitious, successful. She's... Well, she's someone you *could* settle down with—"

"Just not now, with a shotgun at your back."

"And it isn't even Delia holding the shotgun, it's my brother," Andrew agreed wryly.

"But it's still a shotgun," Mike said. "What about her? Does she want the whole marriage thing even if she isn't the one insisting on it?"

"No, not at all," Andrew said, only telling his friend about the age difference then, and Delia's reluctance to have anything to do with him, let alone marry him. "To tell you the truth, it freaked her out when I told her how old I am, and I think it would have been fine with her if she never saw me again. She had plans for having the baby and raising it alone and was okay sticking to those plans. But I've been pushing and she's let me come around, she's been nice about everything. There's no pressure from her, but she hasn't slammed the door in my face, either. Like I said, she's great," he concluded.

"So you *do* like her," Mike said.

"Sure. I *like* her—"

"But *like* isn't the same as being so crazy in love with her that you're jumping at the chance to shuck everything else and stick with her forever."

"I don't know," Andrew said because he didn't want to admit his friend might be right. And because he felt even more guilt over that fact.

"So what're you going to do?" Mike asked.

Andrew shrugged. "I'm doing everything I can to convince Delia to marry me and I'm going to go on doing that."

"Seriously?"

"Seriously."

"Because your brother says you have to?"

"And because I can't be the last straw that broke Hanson Media Group's back. And because…" Andrew shook his head and shrugged his shoulders, hating the sense of being helpless against the tides of fate that came over him. "And because out there in the world there's going to be a kid I made. A kid I'm responsible for. A kid I can't just act like I didn't have anything to do with," he said, voicing something that he'd realized after hearing Delia tell him about her own father and those of Marta and Kyle. After picturing himself turning his back on his own flesh and blood the way they all had and coming to the conclusion that that wasn't the person he wanted to be.

"Are you telling me to rent a tux?" Mike said, half joking, half honestly asking.

"No," Andrew said. "At least not yet. And if it comes to that, you can just wear one of mine."

If it comes to that...

The words echoed in Andrew's mind as he sat there morosely staring at the dark television again.

Would it really come to that? he wondered.

And if it did, could he handle it?

Could he handle putting his bachelor days—and ways—behind him?

Kissing Delia the night before *had* been good, he reminded himself. Better, even, than he remembered kissing her in Tahiti had been.

But kissing was one thing. Putting his bachelor days—and ways—behind him was something else entirely.

And he wasn't confident that he could....

"I don't know. It's all a mess," he said in conclusion then, standing to put a complete end to the conversation. "And now I'd better get to *work*."

"Oh! You scared me!" Delia said in fright when she opened her front door to leave for work and discovered Andrew standing on her porch.

"Adrenaline—better than caffeine for starting your day," he countered. "I was just going to ring the bell."

"What are you doing here?" Delia asked, still in the throes of that adrenaline he'd sent rushing through her. Adrenaline mixed with a dash of pleasure at seeing him again, no matter what the reason and in spite of the fact that she'd been with him until late the night before.

"I want today and tonight," Andrew announced in answer to her question about what he was doing there.

"Excuse me?"

"I want today and tonight," he repeated. "I was headed into the office and I just decided that I want us both to ditch work and spend today and tonight in a speed courtship—"

"Courtship?" She parroted the word that seemed outdated. "As in horses and buggies? You've come a-courtin'?" she teased him, unable to keep from smiling at how silly that sounded.

"No horses or buggies, but that's about it, yeah," he confirmed. "I've come a-courtin'. First date, second date, third date, maybe even the fourth—all rolled into one. Today and tonight."

"You've lost it," Delia decreed.

"I have not," he said, pretending affront. "The way I look at it, we don't have much time. Three months have already gone by. After three more days you still won't marry me," he said as if that were unfathomable, "so I want to speed things up."

"With a speed courtship?"

"Now you're getting it," he said as if she were finally seeing the light.

"And you think that will accomplish what?"

"At best? You'll fall victim to my spell and say you'll marry me."

"Really, you've lost it," Delia said again.

"You promised to spend time with me," he reminded.

"I spent all last evening with you. But today is a workday. For us both. Or aren't you aware that it's bad form not to show up for your fourth day on the job?"

"Today you're more important than the job," he said. "Come on. Run away with me just for today."

"And tonight."

"And tonight—dating needs a night on the town."

"And at worst?" she asked. But when the question put a confused frown on his brow she clarified. "You have some misguided notion that at best I will fall victim to your spell so I'll marry you. And at worst?"

He leaned forward and confided, "We'll get to know each other some more—which you said you would do—and we'll both get a day off work." He straightened up again. "So what do you say?"

The entire exchange had taken place with Delia's old wooden screen door between them and she went on staring at him through it. But even filtered, his appeal didn't diminish. Because there he stood, tall and broad-shouldered, his sun-streaked hair in perfectly artful disarray, his sharp jaw freshly shaven and the rest of his remarkably handsome face looking rested and ready for mischief. Plus he was dressed in a pair of charcoal-colored slacks, a summerweight heather-gray cashmere sweater and a black peacoat that really did make him look too good to resist.

And the longer she studied him, the lower her resistance got.

"I don't know," she hedged when she knew full well that she shouldn't write off work for the entire day and spend it with the man she was beginning to worry was getting under her skin even if she were trying to prevent it.

"Come on," he repeated. "You're the boss, you can do whatever you want. Just call Marta and tell her to take over for the day. I'll make it worth your while," he added temptingly.

So-oo temptingly…

Temptingly enough to make her think out loud. "I suppose I don't have anything on deck that Marta can't do or that can't wait."

"Then you don't have any excuse."

But what she did have, she was afraid, was the same weak spot that she'd had for him in Tahiti. A weak spot she told herself she should be toughening up, not succumbing to.

On the other hand, she never took a day off work. Most weeks, she worked Saturdays, too. And sometimes Sundays. Taking an impromptu day to do nothing but play was just too unlike her not to have it's own allure. Especially when it meant playing with Andrew, who had made her last day in Tahiti more fun than any of the ones that had come before it. Taking a day off to spend with him made it seem like a minivacation.

"I shouldn't," she said, but without much strength.

"Doing what you shouldn't is what makes it all the better," Andrew assured with that touch of devil-may-care that put a special flair in his own brand of charisma.

"I'm dressed for work," she said as if the skirt and sensible shoes she was wearing were steep impediments.

"So change," he said, solving the problem that simply.

But if she did that Delia knew she'd be changing a whole lot more than her clothes. She'd be changing from die-hard workaholic Delia to...

Well, to someone with a little adventure in her soul.

Or at least to someone who just might, for once, do something out of the ordinary. And that felt exhilarating.

It made her feel a little like she'd felt that night in Tahiti.

That night that had gotten her into trouble.

But she was already pregnant, there wasn't a whole lot more trouble she could get into. And she deserved a day off now and then. A day of rest and relaxation. Wasn't Marta telling her that all the time?

Or am I just rationalizing so it doesn't seem like I'm doing this to be with Andrew? she asked herself.

But she didn't want to look too closely at that possibility and ruin the excitement she was feeling over playing hooky for a day, so before she could think more about it, she said, "Okay. Today and tonight. But this isn't a courtship kind of thing," she qualified to make herself feel better. "It's a 'getting to know each other' thing."

Andrew grinned. "Whatever you say. Just pack up

some fancy clothes for tonight—the restaurant I'm taking you to isn't far from my place so we can go there and dress for that. Now can I come inside while you call Marta and change for today or do I have to go rent a horse and buggy?"

"This is *not* a courtship thing," she reiterated more forcefully, pushing her screen door open to let him in.

But his "Uh-huh," let her know he was only humoring her.

Chapter Nine

Andrew took Delia to breakfast at a small waffle shop not far from her house and then they went to the art museum.

Lunch was panini sandwiches at an Italian deli, followed by shopping in some small boutiques before going to the dress rehearsal of a play in which two of Andrew's friends had parts.

After the play they went with the cast for coffee and gelato at a nearby bistro, where Delia learned that Andrew's friends were more interesting than the characters they were performing.

Then Andrew brought Delia back to his apartment to change from casual clothes to less casual. There she got to briefly meet his roommate, who was on his way out as they were arriving, and to see the spectacular view from the ultra-chic digs that Hanson Media Group had provided and paid a designer to decorate.

All in all it was a whirlwind day that didn't end when dusk fell. Instead Delia was led to the opulent guest room to shed her slacks and shirt, and slip into the red lace dress she'd brought with her.

The dress was completely form-fitting over a flesh-colored liner that made it look as if more of her was showing through it than actually was. It also had a stand collar, long sleeves and a hem that barely made it to midthigh. She'd only worn it once before and knew she wouldn't be able to wear it much longer, but for now she could still get it zipped up the side without any difficulty.

Nude-toned hose and a pair of three-inch strappy sandals finished the outfit before she brushed out her hair and twisted it into a French knot at the back of her head. Then she reapplied blush, mascara and lipstick, and added a caramel-hued eyeshadow as a finishing touch for the evening that she warned herself she shouldn't be looking so forward to.

But warning or no warning, after a day of Andrew's unfailingly upbeat, charming company, she just couldn't help it.

He was waiting for her in the living room when she left the guest bedroom. He'd gone from his daytime clothes to a deep brown suit that matched the color of his eyes. A suit so fluid it had to have been handsewn to his own personal measurements. The pale tan shirt and tie beneath it matched in elegant perfection, making him a sensational sight to behold standing in the midst of his impeccable apartment that bore absolutely no resemblance to the fraternity house she'd imagined when he'd told her he had a roommate.

And it struck Delia that culture, breeding and sophistication provided more of an air of maturity than her mother's younger men had ever possessed. She thought that that explained why not only had she not realized in Tahiti that Andrew was so much younger, but also why it had been easy for her to forget their age difference throughout the day, too.

Still, it wasn't something she *wanted* to forget, she warned herself even as his dark eyes seemed to devour her.

"You look fantastic," he said with enough appreciation in his tone and in his expression to make her believe it.

Delia humbly inclined her head. "Thank you. You're not too shabby yourself," she countered.

"Good enough to marry?" he joked.

"Good enough to have dinner with," she amended.

"Damn. I knew I should have gone with the blue suit," he muttered, picking up her coat from where it was draped over a chair and stepping to Delia to hold it for her.

She turned her back to him to slip her arms into the sleeves and caught the reflection of Andrew's face in a framed mirror on the wall in front of her as his eyes dropped to her derriere. Apparently he liked what he saw there, too, because a tiny smile lifted one corner of his mouth before he actually settled the coat on her shoulders.

But even if she hadn't spied him ogling her backside he would have given himself away when he said, "I didn't think it was possible for you to wear anything that beat the sarong, but this dress does."

With her coat in place Delia turned to face him again, pleased with the flattery but beginning to feel a little self-conscious. "Are you going to feed me tonight or not?" she demanded, to change the subject.

"Whatever you want," he answered, swinging an arm in the direction of the door to let her know to go ahead of him.

The restaurant he took her to was in a private club that had a reputation for a membership of only the most elite of Chicago's movers and shakers. Andrew was greeted by name and as the maitre d' did that, two men stepped out of nowhere to simultaneously remove both Delia's coat and Andrew's. Then they were escorted into a dimly lit, wood-paneled enclave where enough space was left between the linen-clothed tables to make sure conversations weren't overheard.

After they'd ordered virgin cocktails and hors d'oeuvres, they were left with menus that looked like leather-bound books.

Andrew didn't open his, he merely set it aside. "They do a beef Wellington that's great. But just about everything here is great."

Delia didn't bother with her menu either, placing it out of the way, too. "Sounds good," she said, more interested in the man she was with than in the food, and wishing that wasn't the case.

But since it was, she focused her attention on him

and said, "How did your brother take the news that you weren't working today?"

"I don't know. I just left him a message," Andrew answered with a smile that said he might enjoy it if he'd irked his brother. "I can always tell him it was business, that I was just doing my job and wooing a potential client."

"Is that what you're doing?" Delia asked, a bit disappointed that that might be the case.

"Have we talked business today?" he countered.

They hadn't. They'd talked about art and movies and books they'd both enjoyed, they talked about other plays they'd seen, and food they liked, but they'd never touched on business. Which, now that Delia realized that, made her feel better again.

"Maybe we *should* talk business," she said, thinking that it might be safer to head in that direction than to continue in the personal vein that had made her like him all the more today.

"Okay, tell me about how Meals Like Mom's came to be."

"I know you haven't been at this long but my work history isn't relevant to selling me advertising."

"I'm not here to sell you advertising," he said as if he were telling her a secret. "Even if that's what I tell my brother, we aren't going to get into that tonight. My brother wants your business. I want more than that."

The room was just the right temperature but his words sent a tiny shiver of goose bumps up her arms anyway. Delia cautioned herself against being too susceptible to this man and his charm and instead answered his question just to get conversation going on a more surface route.

"Meals Like Mom's was sort of an evolution," she said. "It all started when I was fourteen and wanted an expensive lipstick."

"Lipstick? Your business was built on a lipstick?"

"I was a freshman in high school and I got asked to the spring dance by a junior—Damon Simosa—and I didn't think I could possibly be seen with an older man without this lipstick."

"But Peaches didn't have expensive lipstick budgeted in," Andrew guessed as their drinks and appetizers arrived.

"She said she had plenty of lipsticks I could wear. But I had my heart set on this one particular one. I just didn't have the money for it. So I lied about my age and got a job fixing trays with a catering company."

Andrew sampled his virgin daiquiri.

"You really could have had a drink, I don't mind," Delia repeated what she'd told him when he'd ordered the same liquorless drink she had.

"It seems only fair that I abstain if you have to," he said, urging her to taste one of the mushroom caps stuffed with lobster.

After she'd marveled over how good it was, he said, "So at fourteen you went to work for a catering company fixing trays."

"Right. But this is pretty boring stuff, you may not want to hear it."

"You haven't bored me yet," he assured. "And we're talking about your business to appease my brother, remember? If you don't tell me you'll be making a liar out of me. So give me the whole saga of your meteoric rise from tray fixer to company owner."

"It wasn't meteoric," Delia amended with a laugh. "I stayed with the company, basically learning every aspect of the business, saving my money—"

"With the exception of buying expensive lipstick."

"With the exception of buying expensive lipstick, and when the owner decided to sell out, I used what I'd saved, supplemented it with a small business loan, and bought the company—which was Cartwright Caterers then."

The waiter returned and Andrew placed their dinner order. Once he had, he went right back to their conversation. "But unless somebody has led me astray, Meals Like Mom's isn't technically a caterer."

"The longer I did the catering, the more I turned toward organic foods, healthier ingredients, things that were fancy enough for parties or weddings, but that were also not full of preservatives or chemicals. I made sure to put that into my advertising—"

"See? Now we've talked advertising and I'm legitimate," he pointed out, making her smile. "Go on."

"Well, when people hiring me would see that the food was wholesome, too, they started making comments about how they wished they could have every-night dinners catered that way for their families. I thought there might actually be a market for meals that were as good and healthy and hearty as moms made—"

"Not your mom, though."

"No, but meals like I'd often fantasized that my mom might make. So I branched off from the catering business into packaging meals for one to however many. I already had the kitchens, the equipment that we used for the catering end of things, and the accounts with organic food wholesalers, which meant I could keep costs reasonable—that's a big thing when you're up against drive-through windows at fast-food restaurants that are easy to hit on the way home. So mainly it was a matter of packaging, *advertising*—"

"Twice. We're doing good."

"And distribution and delivery. But the idea ended up taking off to such a degree that we closed the catering business and got rid of its more complicated headaches, to concentrate on Meals Like Mom's. And here we are."

Their salads were served then and when their waiter left them alone again, Andrew said, "So you've always been ambitious."

Delia laughed. "Maybe living the way we did in pursuit of Peaches's dream of being a starlet taught me hard work was a better route."

"I admire that," he said.

"But you wouldn't have traded traveling and having a good time," she guessed.

His smile was unashamed. "I have had a good time."

"But now it's nose to the grindstone. Or at least it was for the three days before today," she teased him.

"You could make me a star and send me back to work tomorrow with the advertising accounts of Meals Like Mom's," he challenged.

"Not tomorrow, but it's still under consideration," she said as their entrées were served.

"Glad to hear it. I'll report that. But no more business talk," Andrew decreed, going on to make her laugh with the sordid history of the club that he claimed had been a speakeasy and notorious casino in the 1920s.

Dinner was followed by nightcaps and dessert at a hotel lounge, where a blues singer with a stupendous voice was a nice finish to a day and evening more full than Delia's social life generally was in a year. Only then did Andrew finally agree to take her home.

"Thanks for this," he said as he walked her to her door.

"For what? You were the one to whisk me away, arrange for everything, entertain me and take care of all the details *and* all the checks. It's me who should be thanking you."

"I'm just glad if you had a good time," he said, taking her keys from her hand and unlocking her door before giving them back to her.

He didn't make any move to go beyond the porch, though, standing with his back bracing the screen door open as Delia took only one step inside.

She flipped on the entryway light and then turned to face him again. When she had, it struck her as strange that something about him had changed in just that moment that she'd lost sight of him. His expression was more thoughtful, more open somehow.

"You're an interesting woman, do you know that?" he asked her as his eyes delved into hers and seemed to infuse her with a warmth that protected her from the cool late-night air.

"Oh, I don't think so," she demurred.

He smiled a small smile that seemed to say he knew she would say that. "Hey, how can anyone who had a mother named Peaches be anything but interesting?"

"Peaches was interesting but that doesn't make me interesting by default."

"You're independent, you're a visionary, you're brave and strong and determined. You're different from most women I've met up with. I like that."

"I suppose working women are sort of a novelty in your circles."

"Not only women who work, but women who have any substance. I'm probably not worthy of that."

She could tell he wasn't merely saying that. That he was feeling it, too. But not in any self-pitying way. It was more that he was simply recognizing what he *did* feel.

"I'd give it everything I've got to *be* worthy, though," he added then. "If you married me."

"It doesn't have anything to do with worthiness," she said quietly, again wishing away her own feelings since having the courage to show her a hint of his vulnerable side only made him all the more appealing. "You have a lot to offer. You're personable and sweet and thoughtful and you have a real knack for making everyone around you feel comfortable and appreciated and good about themselves. You're fun and full of energy and I know you're trying hard here, but—"

"I don't want to be one of the dads like yours and

Marta's and Kyle's, Delia," he said so earnestly Delia could tell what she'd told him about her family had impacted him in a way she'd never meant it to. That it had impacted him enough for him to apparently make it his goal *not* to abandon the baby.

But good intention didn't bring with them the same thing that age and experience and hard-earned maturity did. His good intentions allowed Delia to hope for the best when it came to him actually being some sort of father to the baby, but his good intentions weren't enough to convince her to jump into a relationship—let alone a marriage—with both feet. Even though she was surprised to discover a small part of her that almost wanted to.

He smiled down at her after a moment of the silence her thoughts had caused and lightened his tone to joke slightly, as if he knew what she'd been going to say before he'd interrupted her. "I know, I'm Superman *but* there's the age thing, and the 'we're still strangers' thing, and probably more things than you're even telling me. But you could marry me anyway and just in case there's even an ounce of you that's tempted to, I want you to know that I wouldn't make you sorry if you did."

Delia smiled, too. "But I'm not going to marry you," she whispered to ease the blow this time, not admitting that there actually *was* an ounce of her—maybe even more than an ounce—that was tempted.

It concerned her to realize it, and she decided that on that note she should definitely put an end to this day and evening that had actually done what he'd wanted it to do—it had put a crack in her barriers and resolve, and cast some of that special spell that was Andrew's.

"I'd better go in," she said then.

"You *are* in," he pointed out with a nod of his chiseled chin in her direction. "What you really mean is that I'd better go home."

"You'd be uncomfortable sleeping in your car," she joked rather than giving him outright encouragement to leave.

He took a deep breath and sighed elaborately. "Okay, okay, you still won't marry me and I have to go home. I get it."

But he didn't leave. He continued to stand there, staring at her, studying her, looking as if he didn't want to stop.

Then he bent at the waist just enough to meet her lips with his in a kiss that Delia had the impression he'd only intended to be a simple kiss, like the one from the night before.

Only right away it wasn't simple at all.

She didn't know why, whether it was the day they'd just spent together, or the talking they'd done that had brought them closer, or if it was some sort of chemical reaction, but that kiss that she'd been sure had begun as a customary goodbye was suddenly much more.

Delia wasn't even conscious of him moving and yet in an instant Andrew had pulled her nearer. He'd wrapped his arms around her. He was cupping her head as it inched back with the deepening of that kiss.

His lips parted over hers and hers parted in answer, making way for his tongue when it came to trace the edges of her teeth, to greet her tongue tip to tip, to circle and spar and introduce an entirely new element as their bodies pressed front-to-front and his arms tightened around her.

But it wasn't merely Andrew who had altered that initial kiss. Delia discovered herself doing her part, too. Meeting and matching his tongue with her own, playing any game he initiated and initiating a few herself.

She also found her arms somehow around him. Her hands pressed to the breadth of his back. Her nipples hardened to twin peaks at his chest, demanding to be acknowledged, too.

She even began to wonder what would happen if she pulled him inside her house....

Picturing it, she could see herself tugging him across the threshold into the entryway. She could see herself kicking the front door closed behind them. Continuing to kiss him the way she was, only with even more fervor, more passion, more of the urgency that was mounting in her with every passing moment.

But the longer she considered it, the more caution prevailed.

She'd already ventured further than she should have with him today. Tonight. She'd already missed work— something that was unheard of for her. She'd already ignored her responsibilities. She'd already given Andrew hours and hours she shouldn't have given him. She'd already done so many things that were unlike her—not even counting Tahiti. And she knew she just couldn't go on doing that. Doing what went against the grain for her.

So she reminded herself of every reason she absolutely should not be kissing him in the doorway, let alone bringing him inside to do more. She mentally yanked herself out of that spell Andrew had put her under and forced herself to regain some control. She ordered herself to end that kiss rather than urging it on.

It was no easy task. But after another few minutes of that toe-curling kiss, she finally put her hands between them and pushed until Andrew got the message and stopped kissing her.

"I know," he mock-complained in a voice affected by what they'd both just been absorbed by. "Go home."

Delia smiled. "Yes, go home," she confirmed.

"All right, all right. But not happily," he lamented, kissing her forehead before letting her loose.

He butted the screen door away and side-stepped out of its lee, pointing a long finger at her. "But you haven't seen the last of me," he warned before he turned on his heels and really did leave.

And tonight Delia couldn't make herself close the door without first watching him walk all the way to his car and get behind the wheel again.

Because tonight she couldn't refuse herself every last minute of him.

It was something that gave her fair warning that she was treading on thin ice when it came to this man.

But with her lips still singed from the heat of his kiss, the fair warning was difficult to take to heart.

And even more difficult to take to bed with her.

While memories of the kiss?

Those traveled very well....

Chapter Ten

Andrew had been awake many, many mornings at 5:00 a.m. The difference between those other mornings and this one, though, was that he was usually just rolling in from a long night of partying. *This* morning his alarm went off and he needed to roll out of bed. And he decided on the spot that he far preferred 5:00 a.m. as the end of the night rather than the beginning of the day.

But in spite of the fact that he'd only had about three hours sleep, he turned off the alarm, sat up and swung his feet to the floor.

For a moment he propped his elbows on his knees and rested his face in his hands. But only for a moment before he felt himself drifting off again. Then he shook his head like a dog shaking off water and flipped the switch that turned on the overhead light.

Of course it blinded him and he squinted against the pain, blinking repeatedly until he could tolerate the glare. Once he could, he reached for his cell phone on the bedside table, knowing he needed to get into gear.

He had a plan and if he was going to pull it off, he had to get started. Really, really early.

He knew his stepmother wouldn't be awake yet, but that didn't stop him from punching in her number. He required something from her and knowing her, she'd be so glad he was asking for a favor she'd overlook the pre-dawn wake-up.

"Helen? This is Andrew," he said when she answered on the third ring, sounding sleepy and alarmed at once.

"Andrew? What's wrong?"

Of course she would think he was calling with bad news of some kind. It wasn't like him to call her at all, let alone at this hour.

"Nothing's wrong," he assured quickly to allay her fears. "I apologize for waking you but I need something, I need it in a hurry—an incredible hurry—and you know the people and have the connections to help me make it happen."

"I'm sorry, Andrew, I'm groggy. You're sure nothing has happened?"

She seemed to have stalled on that.

"No, honestly, nothing has happened," he assured, feeling slightly guilty when it occurred to him that this call might be bringing up some sort of flashback for her. He wasn't exactly sure of the details of how Helen had been told of his father's death, but his father had had a heart attack at night, at his office, and Helen had been the first one notified.

"I would have waited for a more decent hour if I could have," he said. "I know this must seem insane to you—calling you at five in the morning—but it's important to me and to Hanson Media Group, and in order to do what I want to do, every minute of today will count."

"It's okay," Helen said, beginning to sound more alert. "I'm always here for you. For you and Jack and Evan. Whenever, wherever, whatever."

She was trying. Just as she always had. Trying to help. To be agreeable. To be a parent. A friend. He had to give her points for that. Even if it didn't change his feelings about her.

And in this instance her desire to play a role in his life that neither he nor his brothers had ever accepted her in was going to work to his advantage, so he appreciated it.

"Are you thinking clearly yet?" he asked.

"Better. My eyes are open, anyway," she said with a light laugh. "I'm glad to hear from you at any time. I learned through the grapevine that you'd come back to Chicago. And about the baby…" She faltered over that, as if she might have had second thoughts about saying it once she had. "Can I… Should I congratulate you? Or is it a sore subject? I know Jack has pushed you to marry the woman and you weren't altogether happy about that, but maybe that's changed? Maybe it will all work out?"

She was rambling without so much as taking a breath, and Andrew forced patience he didn't genuinely feel. But then, he'd never felt comfortable with his stepmother, and the harder she tried to connect with him, the more uncomfortable he was.

However, he reminded himself that she could do what no one else he knew could, and so he said, "Helping me meet Jack's requirements is sort of what I wanted to talk to you about. It's what I'm attempting to do. And that's where you come in. Today, at least. And why I'm rousting you out of bed."

Andrew heard what seemed to indicate that she was sitting up and possibly turning on her own lamp.

Then she said, "Okay, what can I do for you?"

Eager. She was so damn eager to please when it came to him or either of his brothers. It was kind of a shame that she hadn't learned yet that things between them all weren't likely to change. That neither he nor his brothers would ever embrace her as a part of their family.

But again, he needed her.

So he jammed his fingers through his hair, sat up straighter and kept his tone level as he laid out his plan.

When he'd finished and Helen had promised to put him in touch with everyone she could to make sure he accomplished what he'd set out to do today, he said, "I'll let you go so you can make those calls for me. I have to get hold of Jack, too."

"If I were you I'd wait until he's been up a while and

had his coffee," Helen cautioned. "I stopped by the office yesterday and he wasn't too happy that you hadn't come in. David was complaining that Evan still hasn't responded to any of their messages, and Jack was saying that if Evan was anything like you, it didn't matter because all they got out of you was three days work and then you'd disappeared."

"In the first place, you know as well as I do that they don't just need Evan in Chicago for manpower, we can't have the reading of Dad's will until he gets here with the rest of us. And in the second place, I didn't *disappear*," Andrew said, taking issue. "I called in. And being with Delia is what he *told* me to do—both for her business and to *do the right thing.*"

"Oh, I didn't mean to make you angry," Helen said in a hurry. "I'm just saying not to call him right now."

"Yeah, okay, I suppose I can wait until office hours," Andrew conceded, knowing that his brother wasn't going to be any too happy to find out that he wouldn't be in today, either....

"Kyle? It's me. Did you give up hope that I'd ever call you back today?" Delia greeted her younger brother on her cell phone.

"Just about," he responded. "I'm in my car, on my way home from work."

"Me, too."

"You, too? It must be, what? Eight o'clock there?"

"My dashboard says eight-o-seven," she informed him.

"What are you doing working so late? Especially on

a Friday night? And in your condition?" Kyle repri-
manded.

"My *condition?*" she repeated with a laugh. "I
played hooky yesterday so I had the stuff I didn't do
then and today's work to do today, too—that's why I
had to stay so late."

"Um-hmm," Kyle said knowingly. "I heard you
actually missed yesterday."

"Marta said she'd talked to you."

"About a lot of things. I understand our boy Andrew
appeared from out of nowhere."

"He appeared from Tahiti, where we left him three
months ago," Delia said.

"Long vacation."

"Apparently until this week he was living the lush
life of a trust-fund baby and a three-month vacation
wasn't unusual," Delia informed her brother, going on
to explain Andrew's job and family situation to Kyle as
she drove.

"He honestly never worked before this week?" Kyle
marveled.

Kyle had begun delivering newspapers from his
bicycle when he was barely ten years old and hadn't had
a gap in his employment history since. It was no wonder
it was difficult for him to believe Andrew had *never* had
a job.

"Honestly," Delia confirmed.

"But he's selling advertising for his family's company now?" Kyle asked as if that redeemed the other
man. To some extent, at any rate.

"Well, that's what he was doing the first three days

this week. Yesterday he was with me and I don't know about today. He could be back in Tahiti by now," Delia said wryly.

"Except that I thought he was hanging around, trying to persuade you to marry him."

"Ah, you and Marta really did talk about a lot of things."

Kyle didn't bother denying it. The siblings had never been secretive with each other. Instead he said, "She told me he's my age and that pushed your negative buttons."

"Because *I'm* not your age," Delia pointed out unnecessarily.

"And because you aren't Peaches," Kyle guessed.

"This would definitely be right up her alley."

"Andrew's a good guy, though. We all liked him in Tahiti."

"I'm not disputing that he's a good guy," Delia agreed, trying not to think too much about just how much of a good guy Andrew seemed to be. Or how much of a good time she had when she was with him. Or how good he made her feel. Or how good he kissed...

"Seems like his being a good guy should carry more weight than his age," Kyle said.

"You're on *his* side?"

"I'm not on anybody's side. I'm just saying that he isn't a creep, it's his baby you're having, and he wants in on the whole thing. Maybe you should cut him some slack."

"He's twenty-eight. He's only held a job for a few days in his entire life. He has a roommate because he travels so much he needs someone else to watch his place. What about that shouts 'ability to make a long term commitment to you'?"

"K.C. did it for me."

K.C. was Kyle's and his wife Janine's five-and-a-half-year-old son. The baby Janine had been pregnant with before she and Kyle had gotten married. The *reason* Janine and Kyle had gotten married.

"You know I didn't think I was ready to get married when Janine turned up pregnant," Kyle continued. "But it was just what I needed to make me grow up."

"Who are you kidding?" Delia said with another laugh. "You wanted to go to the first day of kindergarten in a suit and tie. You were born with an old soul. You were always grown up."

"Andrew didn't strike me as a big baby," Kyle observed.

"Maybe not a *big* one…"

"Come on, he's not a kid."

"But just how much of an adult is he?"

"Adult enough to want to be a husband and a father to his child. That makes him more adult than any of our fathers or any of Peaches's other boy toys."

"In theory Andrew wants to be a husband and a father, but I'm not so sure he's thought about the reality of it. Or the fact that it doesn't end. Or at least isn't supposed to."

"But you aren't even letting it begin."

Delia groaned. "Come on, be on my side."

"How about if I'm on the baby's side?"

Delia had feared that was the route her brother's opinion would take. "I know what you're thinking."

"I'm thinking that I wanted a father," he said decisively and without shame.

"I know, Kyle," Delia muttered compassionately.

"I'm thinking that in one way or another, we all did—even if you hid it better than Marta or I, and even if it didn't come out in you until later in the game," Kyle said, obviously running along the same lines Marta had voiced when she and Delia had discussed this earlier in the week. "And I'm thinking that the father—the real, genuine, father of your baby wants you and wants to *be* a father to your baby, and that you shouldn't blow that off so cavalierly."

Had she blown it off cavalierly? Delia asked herself, feeling guilty suddenly to think that might be the case. To think that her baby might grow up and think and feel the way her brother did and decide she *had* blown off the baby's chance to have a father without giving it serious consideration.

"Come on," she repeated, beseeching her brother's understanding. "Don't be so hard on a pregnant woman."

"Maybe somebody has to be," her brother said gently. "It sounds to me like Andrew is trying, Dealie. Yes, I agree that unplanned pregnancies—especially with somebody you just met for one day on a vacation—aren't the best foundations for marriages. But an honest desire to try to make things work out goes a long way in having it happen. Look at Janine and me. We're happy. We may not have come to our marriage without complications, but we did come to it willing to give it our all, and that's been just as good—if not better—than getting married in some unrealistic haze of hormones."

Wasn't that similar to what Andrew had said the night before? That he'd give it everything he had if she would marry him?

"I don't know, Kyle…." Delia hedged.

"Maybe not, but maybe you should do some more thinking about it. Considering it. And Andrew. Rather than just writing him off," Kyle concluded, again making it clear he and Marta were of a similar mind on the issue.

"You're really being mean to me tonight," Delia complained.

"Not *really*. I just don't want you to make a mistake that you and the baby might regret forever. The baby—and you—deserve at least the possibility of having a second parent in the picture."

"Hmm… I just turned onto my street and it looks like the man in question's car is parked at my curb. He's not in his car but there are lights on inside the house," Delia said, seizing the discovery as a method of not answering her brother's pressure on her to change her decision.

"Does he have a key?" Kyle asked.

"No, he doesn't. Apparently he knows a little something about breaking and entering."

"See? He does have a skill," her brother joked.

"Gr-reat," Delia said facetiously.

"Since you're home and have company, I'll let you

go. But think about what I said."

As if she was going to be able *not* to.

"I'll talk to you soon," she countered before they said goodbye and she turned off her phone.

But as she pulled into her driveway wondering what Andrew had up his sleeve tonight, she realized that her brother's words might have had a stronger impact at that moment, because she was already coming to feel more and more torn.

Torn between what her head was telling her to do—or *not* to do—and the direction she was worried her heart might be beginning to lean.

"But for some reason he *did* break into my house," she told herself out loud just to help keep even a semblance of balance before her heart—and her brother's and sister's opinions—swayed her too much.

Chapter Eleven

As Delia climbed the steps to her porch after having talked to her brother on the drive home from work her emotions seesawed.

On the one hand she wasn't exactly thrilled that Andrew had taken the liberty of getting into her house when she wasn't there. Why would he do such a thing? she wondered, unable not to feel a bit intruded upon as she mentally catalogued if she'd left her bra hanging to dry in the bathroom, if that laundry basket of underwear waiting on the dryer to be folded could be easily seen from the kitchen, if there were dishes in the sink or mail scattered on the countertops or if her unsightly old bedroom slippers were in the living room by some chance.

But on the other hand, she also couldn't help imagining an entirely different scenario from the one in which Andrew discovered she owned a few pairs of granny-pants underwear and wore slippers that should have been thrown away years ago. She couldn't help imagining that he'd found his way into her house when she wasn't there to set up some romantic welcome-home for her tonight. A candlelit dinner, maybe?

Or maybe he was upstairs in her bedroom. His marble statue's body stretched out on her bed, wearing only that pair of blue jeans he'd had on the night he'd arrived in Tahiti that made his rear end look amazing; his broad, honed torso bare, braced on one arm, the biceps bulging mounds of muscle. She pictured that devil's own smile on a mouth that was just waiting to begin again what she'd had such trouble ending the night before....

"Okay, but he *broke* in," she told herself out loud as a reminder she hoped would cool down the internal heat that that vivid image had turned on.

When she reached her front door she tried the handle before putting her key in the lock to see if it was open. It was, allowing her merely to turn it and push the door wide.

"Andrew?" she called before stepping inside, suddenly considering the possibility that her burglar might just drive the same kind of car—as unlikely as it was that a burglar would drive a Jaguar.

But it was Andrew's deep, distinctive voice that answered. From upstairs.

"Follow your leaders."

Her leaders?

Waging a second battle against the fantasy of him laid out on her bed, Delia stepped over the threshold and discovered tiny stuffed animals set one per step all the way up her stairs.

"My leaders," she repeated, assuming the toys were what he was referring to.

She closed the door behind her and set her purse and briefcase on the entryway table. Then, she did as she'd been told, bypassing a bright yellow monkey, a pink bunny, a black-and-white loppy-eared dog, an elephant, a giraffe, a turtle, a dolphin, a camel, a lion and a floppy moose to reach the second floor landing.

Her eyes went immediately to her own room. The door was open—the way she always left it—but there was no light flooding out. Instead a frog, a teddy bear, a fluffy kitten and a buffalo continued across the hardwood floor to the room she had designated as the future nursery.

Light *was* shining from that open door and with her curiosity at peak capacity, she made her way to it.

But it wasn't a semi-nude Andrew she discovered when she did. He was fully clothed—in those jeans she'd been fantasizing about and a plain white T-shirt with the long sleeves pushed to his elbows. And he was standing at the opposite end of a room that was no longer four scarred, lavender walls with uncurtained windows. A room that had been transformed as if by magic into the nursery of her dreams.

"What's this?" she whispered, almost unable to believe what she was seeing.

"What's it look like?" he asked with a quizzical arch of his eyebrows.

Delia didn't rush to answer. Instead she stepped farther into the room and did a very slow pivot to take it all in.

The awful lavender walls were now a soft, creamy color, divided at chair-rail height with a border of baby forest creatures frolicking merrily through trees and bushes and scampering across bubbling brooks. The floor was no longer covered with indoor-outdoor carpeting but now sported a thick shag that matched the color of the walls.

And no longer was the room empty of furniture, either. Now, angled in one corner just to Andrew's left there was the very crib she'd seen in her decorator's catalog—a white crib with each end a high, graceful slatted arc that looked like white rainbows. Now there was a changing table, bureau and armoire that matched the crib. There were softly drawn-back curtains on both sets of windows. There was a toy box and a play table and toys on shelves that lined one wall. There was a rocking chair cushioned in a downy pad near the crib, and a table lamp to one side of it. There were even picture frames awaiting baby pictures.

All together it was serene and beautiful and cute, too. It was whimsical and fun and still well-organized and user-friendly. And she loved it.

Her gaze came full circle to that spot where Andrew stood waiting for her to answer his question.

She wasn't sure if he was worried he might see disapproval of his efforts in her eyes and so couldn't meet them, or if he was simply afraid she'd missed the mobile of the same woodland creatures that frolicked on the wall border, but he glanced away and reached a long index finger to flick the bunny's tail and set the entire mobile into motion.

"You've been busy," Delia understated, finding her voice small and cracked with the same emotion that was flooding her eyes with tears.

"Boy, have I," he said with effect. "Beginning with calling Marta before she was out of bed this morning to tell her what I wanted to do so she would help me get in. She let me borrow her key."

Then he must have realized how emotional this had made her because he said, "This isn't supposed to make you cry."

She *was* crying by then, though, as the tears became too much to contain and rolled down her cheeks. "They're happy tears, if that helps."

"Well, a little, I guess," he answered, closing the distance between them in two strides of those longs legs and taking her into his arms to comfort her.

Powerful arms that pulled her in close to his body where she could rest her cheek against his chest.

She didn't dare stay that way for long. Not when, almost instantly, other emotions found life, too. The kind that had spurred the night they'd spent together in Tahiti, the kind that had erupted during the heated kiss of the previous evening, too.

Struggling to keep control of *something,* Delia blinked back the moisture in her eyes and raised her head from Andrew's well-defined pectorals. "I'm getting your shirt wet," she said, dabbing her damp cheeks with her fingertips.

"It's okay," he assured, but he made way for the arms and hands that came between them and she increased the slight distance by standing straighter and taking another look around at the room.

Even on second sight it took her breath away.

"How did you do this?" she asked.

"You told me you'd hired a contractor and a decorator to do your remodel, and I saw the decorator's card near your kitchen phone when we were in there the other night. I recognized it because my stepmother has used that same designer. And I knew which room you were planning to use as the nursery—"

"I didn't think you were that interested."

He merely frowned at that notion and continued with his explanation. "So when I got this idea, I enlisted my stepmother. I figured the decorator would do anything for her—Helen is a valued customer—and I was right. One call from dear old stepmom and your designer dropped everything today to work solely with me."

"Impressive. But my decorator couldn't have done all this."

"No, but she did know what you were leaning toward in here when it came to the colors and furniture. And she could put me in touch with your contractor. I did some wheeling and dealing—"

"With the contractor?" Delia interrupted Andrew a second time in astonishment. "The contractor is who's holding us up until the end of the month. You didn't get him in here *today*, did you?"

"I did. Him and his whole crew."

"How?"

"I told you, wheeling and dealing. I found some common ground and used it. He's a motorcycle buff. I happened to own a vintage Harley-Davidson that I used as a bribe."

"You got him to do this by promising to let him ride your motorcycle? That's all it took?" Delia asked.

"Not quite. He's now the proud new owner."

Delia hadn't thought that Andrew could surprise her more than he already had, but that accomplished it. "You sold him a vintage Harley-Davidson motorcycle in order to get him over here today?"

"Sold would not be the right word. Let's call it an incentive gift."

Delia's eyes widened this time. "You *gave* it to him? What must that have been worth?"

"This," Andrew said with a nod to the room in general and without missing a beat, stunning her.

Then he said, "I'm not fooling around, Delia. I told you, I'm willing to do anything and everything it takes."

For the first time, Delia believed him.

And something about that made her tear up again.

But she didn't want to cry anymore so she went back to what they'd been talking about before the motorcycle issue.

"Still, you did this in one day?"

"I had a whole parade of workers waiting around the corner while I watched your place from up the street first thing this morning. The minute you left for work, we moved in. Painting came first so gigantic fans could dry the walls, and then we went from there."

Delia glanced at the evidence of his work, thinking about the effort that had to have gone into accomplishing this. "I think you're kind of amazing."

"What? Only *kind of?*" he joked.

But before Delia could respond the doorbell rang.

"Pizza," Andrew informed her. "I've had next to nothing to eat since I got up at five this morning and I was beginning to think you'd never come home tonight, so I ordered delivery. I'll go get it, you kick off your shoes and sit down, we'll eat up here and break the room in."

Apparently he'd taken command today and was still in that mode. But Delia didn't mind. Actually, it was nice....

While Andrew was downstairs, Delia forced herself to leave the nursery just long enough to use the bathroom and make sure her hair was still caught neatly in its ponytail, her mascara hadn't run and that the simple black slacks and red sleeveless shell sweater she'd worn for casual Friday weren't too wrinkled. Then she did remove her black flats to toss them into her own bedroom before returning to the nursery in her bare feet.

She took away the two tiny chairs that were pushed into the kid-sized play-table so they could use it for their dinner and sat cross-legged on the floor to continue to study Andrew's handiwork until he rejoined her.

"You look like a little kid sitting there," he said with a laugh at her when he did.

"You're the kid," she countered. But she was only teasing him because as she watched his approach with their dinner in hand, it occurred to her that she was seeing him in a new light. One that didn't count the years difference in their ages. One that made her think that maybe there was more to him than she'd given him credit for.

He deposited their meal on the play-table and sat on the floor, too.

"You must be exhausted," she said.

"I think I'll survive," he assured.

Endless energy—an advantage of his youth, Delia thought as she doled out the salads, opened the pizza box and handed him a soda can.

"So," he said once they were both situated with full plates of food. "Is everything okay or do you want to make changes? Because it's all right if you—"

"It's perfect. I don't want to change a thing," Delia said without the need to even consider the possibility. "I still just can't believe you did it."

"Hey, I had to do something to show up the esteemed Damon Simosa."

His reference to the high school boy she'd told him about the night before made Delia laugh in spite of the bite of pizza she'd just taken.

"After all," he continued in the same vein, "I don't see you doing menial labor to buy lipstick to wear for me, so I'm just trying to figure out how I can rate. Or is it only older men who do it for you?"

"Apparently it isn't *only* older men," she said point-edly, tossing another glance at the nursery. "But there have been only older men until you, now that I think about it."

"Really?"

Delia nodded. "'Fraid so."

"On purpose?" Andrew asked after a drink of soda to wash down salad.

"Yes."

"How much older are we talking about?"

"There's been a pretty wide range," she hedged.

"Among the hundreds you've been involved with?" he teased.

"I'm guessing *hundreds* is closer to your number than to mine."

Andrew toasted her with his soda can as if to concede.

"Honestly? You've been with hundreds of women?"

"Either the light in here is bad or you just lost all the color in your face," he said with a grin that was too endearing not to get to her. "No, I haven't been with *hundreds* of women."

"How many *have* you been with?" Delia persisted.

"Probably more than my share. But it isn't as if I keep score."

"How many have you been seriously involved with? Because those are the ones who count. Not people you've seen casually now and then."

Andrew took another slice of pizza, since he'd polished off the first.

"Ones I've been seriously involved with…" he repeated. "In that case, I'm a virgin."

"You haven't been seriously involved with *any-one*? Ever?"

"If I'm assuming that by seriously involved you mean have I been with anyone for a long period of time, considered marriage and proposed, then no. You're the first to hit two out of those three."

"Oh, dear," Delia breathed, a little alarmed to learn that just when she thought she was seeing more depth in him she might be mistaken.

Andrew must have noticed her concern because he gave her a reassuring smile.

"It isn't as if I've been down on marriage or anticommitment or anything. I just haven't stayed in one place for any extended period of time, and once you've been gone for months and you call the person you were dating before you left, well, you usually find that they've moved on."

"But being gone for months was a matter of traveling for pleasure. You *could* have stayed in one place long enough to have a relationship if you had wanted to," Delia reasoned.

"I guess I never met anyone who inspired that in me. There were a few women I asked to come along on trips with me, if that helps. Women I liked well enough to want things to continue with them. If they'd come, who knows? Those relationships might have developed into something serious. But no one ever took me up on the offer."

"Not many people have the kind of freedom you've had," Delia pointed out. "And when whoever you asked to go along couldn't leave for months, apparently you packed up and went anyway. Rather than staying around to let the relationships develop."

Andrew watched her face, a bare hint of a smile playing about his lips as if she amused him. Then, after a moment, he said, "And what are you thinking? That I'd do that with you? That I'd get a notion to take off, ask you to, too, and if you wouldn't, I'd go anyway?"

"It seems possible," Delia admitted, worrying about that exact thing.

"Okay, I'm guilty of never having been more than infatuated with anyone, so yes, I packed up and went anyway," he conceded. Not on the defensive, though. More as if he were clarifying things for her. "But what I've done in the past doesn't mean it's what I'll do in the future. It only means it's what's already happened and what's already happened with everyone else has never been too serious. But now what's happening between us *is* serious and that changes everything that will happen from here on."

Did he honestly consider what was happening between them serious? And if so, why? Was it only because of the pregnancy or were there feelings that were going beyond infatuation that were making it serious in spite of the baby?

Delia couldn't bring herself to ask. Or maybe she just couldn't bring herself to hear the answer. But he did get a gold star for the fact that he was approaching their relationship as something of more importance than any he'd had before.

"So what about you?" he said then, tossing the ball back into her court. "Not hundreds of guys, but no husband or real commitment that I've heard about for you, either. And you've had more time at it," he added jokingly, successfully lightening the tone.

"No, no husband. Or serious commitments," she answered, realizing that she didn't have a whole lot of room to judge Andrew's failure to commit when she'd never done it herself. And feeling slightly better about his history when she considered that.

"But there have been three guys who were long-term," she added, seizing her only claims to even flirting with permanence. "And one of those might have gone the long haul if we hadn't been at different stages of our lives at the time."

Delia had finished eating so she repositioned herself to lean her back against the solid base of the crib for support.

Andrew had another slice of pizza. "And all three guys were older than you?"

"They were. The first guy was five years older and the third guy was eight years older."

"And you didn't marry them because…"

"It didn't get that far with either of them. They were both just guys I saw for extended periods of time— fifteen months and eighteen months respectively—until things just fell apart the way they do, and we knew the relationships *weren't* going anywhere so we called it quits."

"Then there's the second guy," Andrew reminded. "You skipped him, so he must have been the close-to-serious one and the oldest."

Delia laughed at the accuracy of his guess. "You're good," she said as if granting him an award.

"How old and how close to serious?"

"Daniel was seventeen years older than I was."

Andrew's brows headed for his hairline. "*Seventeen* years older?"

Delia nodded. "And don't give me any armchair father-figure analysis," she warned.

"*Seventeen* years?" Andrew repeated as if that were begging for comment.

"I was twenty-six, he was forty-three. He was well-educated, suave, sophisticated, established in his career, stable. He knew what he wanted and how to go about getting it—"

"And what he wanted was you?"

"He'd reached his career and financial goals. He was ready to settle down, get married, have a family, really devote himself to the next phase of his life."

"With you."

"With me," Delia said, feeling the twinge of sadness she always felt when she thought of or talked about Daniel.

"But I assume you didn't feel the same about him," Andrew said.

"I really liked him. I enjoyed his company. We had a lot in common and if the timing had been better I think we would have had a future together. But like I said, we were at different stages of our lives—because of the *age thing*." She emphasized the phrase both she and Andrew had used frequently since discovering their own discrepancies in that department.

"Actually," she went on, "it was an age-*related* thing. While Daniel's career was on cruise control, I was just getting Meals Like Mom's going and I was determined to make it work—that meant late hours, weekends, whatever it took. Daniel was a strict nine-to-fiver by then and he wanted someone to be at home when he was, someone whose job came second. But mine came first at that point and so we ended up saying goodbye."

Andrew had finished eating and he crawled on all fours like a big jungle cat until he reached her side. Once he was there, he did an athletic sort of spin that landed him sitting next to her with his back against the crib, too. He took her hand in his, weaving their fingers together before resting them on his thigh.

Studying them, he said, "That isn't the same as you and I, you know."

"No, I don't know that," Delia answered, glancing at his striking profile. "Meals Like Mom's operates with or without me at this point. I keep late hours because I want to, not because I have to anymore. When the baby comes I plan to keep work to a minimum, to delegate, to set up my office so the baby can come to work with me. I plan to do everything I need to to be a full-time mom. It's what I want to do now. It's where I am in my life. But you… You'd still be on a beach in Tahiti if it had been your choice. And even though it hasn't been your choice and you're here now, it isn't a sure bet that you'll stick to this course. Especially when it wasn't a course you were ready to be on—and that goes for the job and for the baby. Definitely different stages of life," she concluded.

Andrew shook his head, calmly denying that. "I think that the only thing that really matters is that we're here now—regardless of what got us here. You didn't plan this and neither did I. You've had a little longer to accept it and adjust to it than I have, but I think I've come up to speed pretty quick. I won't tell you that I'm still not having moments when I feel sort of overwhelmed. But I'm dealing with it. And the point is, we're sitting together in our baby's room—*our* baby's room. Same time. Same place. Same stage of life— we're going to be parents. You've embraced that. I'm in the process of embracing it. But that slight discrepancy doesn't put us far apart. And that's what's important."

He went from looking at their hands to looking her in the eyes again. To smiling a smile that was even more endearing, more irresistible than the earlier one.

"And when it comes to our pasts," he added, "think of it this way—I don't have any baggage or war wounds to rear up and cause trouble for us. I don't have any preconceived suspicions or mistrusts or expectations that you're going to do me wrong the way someone else did. And it doesn't seem like you do, either. That puts us on a pretty level playing field in that department, too. So age thing or no age thing, again—it seems to me that we're at about the same stage of life."

He could be very persuasive. And it didn't hurt that all during that heartfelt speech he'd been stroking her hand with sensual brushes of his thumb. Putting her qualms to sleep even as he awakened little shards of glitter in her veins.

He raised her hand to his mouth then, kissing it gently, sweetly, before he looked into her eyes once more with such earnestness that it gave her confidence in everything he'd just said. It caused her to think that maybe she could trust it. Trust him. Such earnestness that, for the first time, she actually had a glimmer of hope that things between them really might work out.

But before she could tell him any of that, he kissed her and turned those little shards of glitter to bright, sparkling diamonds. Sparkling diamonds of desire that seemed to have been waiting just below the surface since he'd kissed her the night before.

And all Delia could do was kiss him in return. All she wanted to do was kiss him in return. Give herself over to it, to him, suddenly.

She raised her free hand to the side of his face, slightly rough with the day's growth of beard, drinking in the feel of whiskers and warm, taut skin over the sharp angles of that face she could see in her mind even though her eyes were closed.

His lips were parted over hers and she willingly parted hers, too. Willingly greeted his tongue when it came to toy with hers in that oh-so-sexy way he had, tip to tip, chasing circles, sparring just a little.

Andrew let go of the hand he held, wrapping one arm around her to bring her nearer, and slipping his other hand behind her head. With more aplomb than she would have expected him to have at such a thing, he removed the clip that held her hair in a ponytail and combed his fingers through her pale blond locks.

It made her secretly smile inside to think that he'd wanted her hair loose and had taken the initiative to free it. She only wished she had the courage to take that same initiative when it came to his T-shirt. The T-shirt that stood between her other hand at his back and the feel of his bare skin beneath it.

She was brave enough to caress that broad back, though. To massage it and explore every rise and fall of muscles she remembered ogling as they'd snorkeled in Tahiti—honed and tanned and gleaming with wetness...

Had she been the first to open her mouth even wider than his? To deepen that kiss? To take it up another notch?

Maybe. Not that it had been premeditated. It was just that picturing him in Tahiti, having him there with her now, holding her, kissing her, was turning her on with such speed her thoughts couldn't keep up.

Andrew could though.

With their mouths still locked and tongues still tantalizing each other, he lowered them both to lie on their sides on the thick mat of new carpeting. His body ran the length of hers but with enough of a separation to make her wish there wasn't one.

She felt her nipples knot and push against the confines of her lacy bra as if reaching out to close some of that distance between them. Her back arched all on its own in silent plea, bringing those tight crests into scant contact with his pectorals. Scant enough that it didn't seem as if it would arouse him even more. But a quiet groan rumbled in his throat and he seemed unable to resist drawing a hand down her side, to the hem of her sweater where he slipped underneath it.

Oh, better still!

Warm and big and strong—that was how his hand felt on her bare rib cage before he let it rise higher. High enough to encompass her straining breast.

It was Delia who moaned then. She couldn't help it. She'd been aware of the fact that pregnancy had rendered her breasts more sensitive, but she'd had no idea just how sensitive. She actually writhed beneath his touch, pushing herself more deeply into his palm, begging him with her body to get that bra out of the way, to give her the full, unfettered sensation.

Which was what he did. Sliding fingertips first inside that cup, replacing it with that hand she was in awe of as it kneaded and massaged and explored the nipple that stood proudly out to meet him.

Andrew rolled her to her back and came to lie half on top of her then. Mouths were wide and seeking and growing more insistent by the minute. Both of Delia's arms were around Andrew and her fingers were digging into his back, urging him on.

And on he went, insinuating his leg between hers, pressing the proof of what she was stirring in him against her thigh, raising his leg high enough to awaken that portion of her body as well.

He ended their kiss then, at the same time his hand left her breast long enough to raise her sweater so that he could take that yearning orb into the hot cavern of his mouth. To suck and knead and flick the kerneled crest, to only lightly nip at it with careful teeth, to tug and tease until Delia was nearly wild with the need for even more.

More of him that merely plunging her own hands underneath his shirt to his naked flesh didn't satisfy. More of him that merely flexing into the juncture of his legs didn't complete. More of him in every way...

But just when she wanted more, she got less.

Slowly, as if it was the fight of his life, Andrew stopped. One final, deep pull of her breast into his mouth and he released it, kissing her stomach as he replaced her bra. One final pulse of his knee into her most private spot, of his most private spot against her, and he took his leg away. Two very, very cautious fingers at the hem of her sweater tugged it down over her exposed torso again.

"I want to do this," he said then, his voice deep and gravely, confirming his claim. "But I won't. Not again. Not until you marry me."

"Oh sure, take me to the brink and then give me an ultimatum," Delia joked, staring up into that exquisitely handsome face, into those dark, penetrating coffee-bean eyes.

He smiled crookedly. "Whatever it takes."

He sat up and tugged her to sit up, too. Then he got to his feet and helped her to hers.

"Marry me, Delia," he ordered forcefully.

A flood of things went through her mind. Her conversation with her brother and the points he'd made. The nursery they were standing in and all Andrew had done to finish it. The lengths Andrew had gone to in so many ways to persuade her to make a go of things between them. All he'd said himself and the points he'd made—better points even than Kyle's.

And it suddenly occurred to Delia that maybe she should give Andrew the benefit of the doubt. That maybe she should swallow her pride about the differences in their ages. That maybe, like that night in Tahiti that had been like no other night of her life, she should throw caution to the wind. That she should give in to what he wanted. To what Marta and Kyle thought she should do in providing her child with the father none of the McCrays had been allowed. That she should stop suppressing her own feelings for this man who never left her thoughts, who she wanted with every ounce of her being no matter how she denied it. That maybe, she should take the leap of faith....

"What if I say okay?" she tested.

"Okay, you'll marry me?"

Delia nodded. Tentatively, but she nodded.

Andrew's responding smile was a bit lopsided. "You'll make me a happy man," he said softly.

"Will I really?"

"You really will."

Still Delia hesitated, hoping, praying, that she was doing the right thing. For herself. For Andrew. For the baby.

But then she said, "Okay. I'll marry you. If you're sure..."

Chapter Twelve

The collar was too tight. It was choking him.

Andrew ran his index finger around the inside of it and stretched his neck.

No, there was plenty of room. Maybe it was the tie.

He loosened it but that didn't help either.

"Dammit!" he muttered under his breath, not wanting his voice to travel outside of Delia's downstairs bathroom where he'd just dressed and was on the verge of going out to greet his family and the judge his brother had arranged for to perform the ceremony.

The wedding ceremony.

It was Saturday evening, a week and a day after Delia had agreed to marry him. A whirlwind week in which he'd had to make up the time he'd missed the week before that at work *and* help arrange for tonight's wedding. A week in which he'd hardly had time to think.

But now here he was, on the verge of actually getting married.

And he felt as if he were being choked by the collar of the white silk shirt and tie he had on under his best Italian suit. Even though neither the collar nor the tie were anywhere near to choking him.

Was it the idea that he was getting married that was really doing it?

Married. He'd be married. Married, with a job and a kid on the way.

And he just kept thinking that this was going to be his life from now on—up every day at the same time to go to the same place to do the same things before he came home each night to a wife and a kid and that whole bucket of responsibilities. No more hopping a plane for places unknown when the mood struck. No more free and easy living when he *was* in town. No more lying on a beach for endless days until he was good and ready to go home, regardless of how long that took. No more random pursuit of any and every woman who caught his eye just to see if he could make the conquest.

No more life.

At least no more of life as he'd known it. And enjoyed it. And wanted it to continue.

"Not what you're supposed to be thinking half an hour before your wedding," he lectured himself with a glance up from the vanity to the mirror above the sink as he put the folded white silk square into his breast pocket.

But he didn't seem able to stop the thoughts.

Thoughts about how his entire life had changed and was changing in ways he hadn't been prepared for it to change. Ways he wasn't sure he was prepared for it to change now. Thoughts about the fact that he hadn't had a choice in any of this. About the fact that a part of him felt as if he might never have another free choice at all. Ever. Not another choice that wouldn't have to be made with a wife in mind. And what she wanted and approved of and consented to and wouldn't be hurt by. Not another choice that wouldn't have to be made with a kid in mind...

Choking. There was the choking sensation again.

Obviously not the shirt or the tie. Obviously the situation.

But there was no way out. Not this time. This time he had to stick around. He had to marry Delia. He had to work for a living. He had to be a father....

The walls of the bathroom seemed to close in on him. The room suddenly seemed too small a place for him to be shut up in.

Too small a room.

Too tight a collar and tie.

"Get a grip," he told his reflection. "You can do this. Last-minute jitters—that's all you have. Everybody gets them."

Of course not everyone took a job they didn't want and got married because their family forced them to.

Never in his entire twenty-eight years of living—

including since his brother and uncle had dumped the job and the ultimatum and the pressure to marry Delia on him—had he wanted so badly to run....

A knock on the bathroom door startled him to such an extent that his body jolted as if he'd had an electrical shock.

"It's me," his roommate announced from outside. "You all right in there?" Mike asked.

Andrew didn't feel all right. But he said, "Yeah. Sure."

Mike apparently knew him well enough not to believe that because after a moment's pause, his roommate's voice came again in a confidential whisper, "Hey, man, it'll be okay."

Andrew laughed a mirthless laugh and opened the door a crack. "Easy for you to say."

"I know. But it's the truth," Mike assured. "Delia's great and you like her. Everything else will fall into place."

"Is there a manual for best men that tells you what to say?"

"Nah, I mean it," Mike claimed. "I was just upstairs and I got to see her. If you don't want her, I'll take her."

That made Andrew chuckle more genuinely. "She looks nice?"

"Too good for you," Mike goaded.

"There's never been any question about that," Andrew answered wryly.

"Seriously—are you gonna make it? You look kind of green around the gills."

"I'm fine," Andrew lied.

"Then I'm supposed to tell you it's time to get started."

Suddenly there was such a knot in Andrew's throat that he couldn't speak. He merely nodded and closed the door, trapping himself inside again and suddenly finding that preferable to the idea of leaving the bathroom to face what he was about to face.

"What are you going to do?" he whispered to his reflection as if he were challenging someone else. "Are you going to leave Delia standing at the altar while you hide in the bathroom?"

He didn't know why, but hearing her name when Mike had said it and again now that he said it himself, thinking about her, actually helped.

Delia.

He never had these feelings when he was with her. He felt great when he was with her. He felt as if he could be with her forever. That was not only okay, but also a good thing.

Delia—just keep thinking about her....

He did have fun with her, he reminded himself. He could be himself around her. He could talk to her, trust her, tease her, joke with her. He could relax with her. Totally and completely.

Oh, yeah, it helped to think of Delia.

She was beautiful, too, his friend was right about that. He could stare at her for hours and not get tired of the way she looked. One flash of those big baby blue eyes and he felt as if the sun had come out from behind clouds. And she had a tight little body that didn't quit.

Plus, she was nice. Sweet. Pleasant. Smart. And he was hot for her. Hell, he'd just about gone out of his mind keeping his hands off her this past week.

But marriage? Shouldn't marriage be based on more than what amounted to a strong attraction? Shouldn't it be based on feelings people had for each other?

Okay, he was headed for dangerous territory again, he warned himself.

Just think about Delia. Only Delia...

Besides, he reasoned, it wasn't as if he didn't have any feelings for her. He did. He even thought he cared for her. In a way that he'd never cared for any other woman.

"So maybe Mike is right about that, too. Maybe it will all be okay," he said.

Hell, it was going to have to be because he couldn't get out of this now.

Just think about Delia, he repeated. Just think about Delia....

And that's what he did.

Steadfastly.

To get himself out the bathroom door.

Where all the eyes on all the guests seated in her living room waiting for the ceremony to begin suddenly turned towards him.

And if there had ever been a time he'd actually considered booking it the hell out of someplace, it was at that moment.

But he didn't do it.

He tried to smile.

He moved into place beside Mike.

And he waited for his bride.

"Congratulations, Andrew. It was a lovely wedding."

Andrew had avoided his stepmother all evening but she was standing with his brother Jack and his Uncle David when David motioned for him to join them, so he couldn't put off talking to her any longer.

He also couldn't help stiffening up when she squeezed his arm and raised up to kiss his cheek.

"Wouldn't it be more apropos to say 'Thanks for taking one for the team'?" he responded snidely.

"Oh, I hope not. I know everything that's come about for you in the last two weeks has been thrust upon you to a great degree, but I really like Delia and I think she'll be good for you. I would hate to believe that's honestly how you feel about her or about marrying her," Helen said.

Andrew's late father's widow wasn't the stereotypical-looking trophy wife. She was attractive but not in any overblown way, and she was nothing if not impeccably tasteful. But Andrew's remark had caused her flawlessly made-up face to sober into a forlorn-looking frown that, when Andrew had been a teenager, would have pleased him.

Now he just felt guilty for the petty comment. Not because it had been an ungracious way to accept congratulations from Helen, but because Andrew regretted making such a tasteless comment when it came to Delia. She didn't deserve that.

"You did the best thing," David praised, taking up where Helen had left off. "All the way around. For yourself, too. At least I think that's what you'll come to see in time even if it isn't clear to you now."

"Finding good women has only improved David's and my life," Jack concurred with a glance in the direction of the buffet table where Jack's own bride, Samantha, and David's former personal assistant and new wife Nina were chatting amiably.

"Might have been nice to be able to take *my* good woman on a honeymoon," Andrew countered pointedly, since his brother and uncle had both vetoed that notion.

"We know your pattern too well," Jack said. "If we let you out of here for a honeymoon it'd be the last we saw of you for who knows how long. Besides, you just came back from a three-month vacation and now you have a job to do."

"You did terrific at work this week, though," David added, clearly to soften the blow of Jack not mincing words. "That new chewing gum account is a big one. It's going to help."

"Don't tell me you even managed to get a new advertiser this week while planning the wedding?" Helen inquired.

Andrew thought he knew where that was headed. Helen had been expressing an unusual interest in the business lately and it seemed to him that she might well want more involvement. She never had liked being excluded. From anything.

But when it came to the company, that was the way

it was and Andrew wished she would get used to it. She was his late father's trophy wife and nothing more. And she'd never *be* any more. Not in the eyes of Andrew or his brothers and not when it came to Hanson Media Group, either.

He wasn't in the mood for it tonight, however, and assuming his brother, uncle and stepmother had summonded him to give him the family pat on the back for doing what they'd wanted him to do, he figured he could make his exit from their little gathering.

With that in mind, rather than addressing Helen's comment about the new account, he said, "I should get back to Delia."

"Wait," Jack said to delay him. "We've finally heard from Evan."

That did spur Andrew's interest.

"Finally," David repeated with a full measure of his own irritation over the middle Hanson brother's tardiness in responding to every attempt to contact him.

"I got an e-mail from him just before leaving home tonight," Jack continued. "He'll be in Chicago Thursday. I called the estate lawyer the minute I got the e-mail and arranged for the reading of the will."

"Again—let me just say *finally*," David said.

"When will it be?" Andrew asked.

"Friday morning. The attorney is coming to the office to make it convenient for us. We can all meet in the conference room," Jack said.

"And we really need to get your father's will read," David pointed out. "We've gone too long with things up in the air waiting for you and Evan. That's another reason we couldn't have you taking off on a honey-moon—we knew Evan had to get back to us any time now, and then we could get this all taken care of."

"Hanson Media Group first and foremost," Andrew muttered like a fight song.

"Things do need to be settled," Helen said in a con-ciliatory tone of voice.

Which, for no rational reason, just rubbed Andrew wrong even when he knew she was only trying to make nice the way she always did, and that they were all right and the will did need to be read so the company and everyone connected to it could proceed from there.

But still, he reacted to the irritation he was feeling rather than to the logic of it all. "Well, you know I'll be there. You've all made sure of that. So if that's it, I really should get back to Delia."

"That's it," Jack confirmed.

This time it was David's hand that reached out to take Andrew's arm and halt his retreat. "Make the best of this, Andy," he said. "You won't be sorry."

Delia had come into Andrew's sight just then and seeing her helped to smooth the inexplicable rough edges that had developed during his talk with his family.

So instead of saying anything to his uncle's words of wisdom, he merely nodded as if he were taking the advice to heart before excusing himself and heading for his wife of two hours.

It was after twelve that night when Delia closed the door on the last wedding guest. Andrew was standing right behind her and once the lock was securely in place he proved just how close behind her he was by reaching over her head to brace his weight on his hands as if to prevent the door from opening again to let anyone else in.

Delia could have slipped out from under the archway his body provided but she just wearily dropped her forehead to the carved oak instead.

Andrew kissed the back of her neck, left fair game because her hair was caught up and away from it in a classic French knot.

Then he said, "When my uncle offered to have the wedding at his apartment I turned him down because I thought it would be nice to be married here, in the house that means family to you. It didn't occur to me that that meant we wouldn't be able to slip away when we wanted to."

Delia laughed. "Not only the bride and groom, but the hosts, too. Still, it *was* nice to have it here."

She used what little space was between them to turn around so that her back was to the door and she could look up at him. "Hi," she said as if this were the first time she'd had the opportunity to greet him.

He dipped down to place a miniscule kiss on her lips before answering. "Hi."

Another kiss sent a wisp of warmth through Delia before Andrew raised up and peered into her eyes. "I didn't even get a chance to tell you how beautiful you look."

Delia smiled. She'd fallen in love with her dress the moment she'd seen it at the bridal shop—it was an ankle-length white satin A-line with a lace overlay that reached higher than the sweatheart-shaped bodice that ended just above her breasts, giving a peek-a-boo effect before the lace made a scalloped, off-the-shoulder neckline itself. But she was pleased to know that Andrew liked it, too.

"Your expression brightened up so much when you first saw me I sort of got the idea," she demurred anyway.

"One look at you—the antidote for wedding jitters."

He kissed her once more.

"Did you have wedding jitters?" she asked when that kiss that lasted only slightly longer ended.

"Didn't you?"

She smiled again. "Some," she confessed, unwilling to tell him that she'd been awake the entire night before, hoping she wasn't making a mistake and that this would work for him, for her, and for their baby. But the most she would add as an explanation for her own admission of nerves was, "This has all happened pretty fast."

"And yet some things haven't happened fast enough," he countered with a voice full of innuendo. "At least not fast enough the *second* time…"

That was true enough. After turning her on that night in the nursery and every night they'd been together all week, Andrew had still left her unsatisfied. And with all those pent-up desires just below the surface, Delia took her hands from where they'd been behind her since she'd turned to face him and used them to loosen his tie.

"You were the one who gave the ultimatum, not me," she reminded. "*Not until you marry me*—I believe those were your exact words. And all this last week, you said you wanted to wait. So we waited."

This time it was Andrew who smiled. A wickedly sexy smile that let her know the wait was over. "I was just too afraid that if you got what you were after from me I'd never get you in front of the judge tonight."

Delia took a deep breath and sighed it out resignedly. "True, you might not have," she deadpanned, unfastening his collar button. "I did only agree to this for one reason."

"I knew it!"

"I'm sorry you had to find out this way."

"With you undressing me?"

She *had* unbuttoned his shirt to the middle of his chest.

"Shall I do them up again?" she asked.

"I wasn't complaining," he whispered in her ear, turning up the heat in her another notch with his breath against her skin.

She undid two more of his buttons.

"You looked pretty fantastic yourself tonight," she told him as she did.

Andrew bent low enough to kiss first one of her bare shoulders and then the other.

"So you approved?" he inquired.

"Mmm. Very much," she breathed, leading with her chin to place a kiss underneath his. "Even Kyle and Janine commented on the difference between how you looked tonight and in your beachwear in Tahiti."

Delia's brother, sister-in-law and nephew had flown in for the wedding so that Kyle could give Delia away.

"Little did they know that under these pants I'm wearing bright orange tiger-striped Speedos."

Delia laughed yet again. "Liar. You didn't even wear Speedos in Tahiti."

"Maybe you should check to be sure," he suggested lasciviously as he traced the edge of her scalloped neckline with his nose and sent tiny shivers all through her.

"You want me to take off your pants in the entry-way?" she demanded as if the idea scandalized her.

Andrew mimicked her earlier sigh. "I suppose there are more appropriate places."

"Like the beach."

He took a turn at laughing, too.

Then he kissed her again, this time with his mouth open wide, his tongue running rampantly in to meet hers, and with no doubt left that he'd spent this last week struggling with celibacy as much as she had.

When he ended the kiss, though, he did a push-up off the door and took one of her hands to tug her away from it, too. "No beaches near enough tonight," he decreed, using his free hand to flip off the lights from the main panel near the door. "I guess we'll have to use the bedroom."

"Novel idea," Delia said as he led her up the stairs.

She couldn't resist peeking at his terrific derriere along the way. He really had looked remarkable tonight and watching him even from a distance when he wasn't by her side had only made Delia wish they *could* have started their wedding night earlier. Because of all the things she worried about, a lack of attraction to him was not one of them.

Her bedroom was lit by candles on either side of the bed when they arrived there—something Delia had no doubt her sister had done before leaving shortly before.

"Marta," she said in answer to the quizzical glance Andrew shot to her when he saw them.

But that was the last bit of attention he paid to the lighting, taking Delia to the foot of the queen-sized bed that had also been turned down for them, facing her at the same time he pulled her nearer and kissed her again.

A bedroom kiss. Different than those in the entryway. Different than any they'd indulged in during the week leading up to this moment. His mouth came to hers with an instant passion, open and seeking, hungry and bold.

Not that Delia had any reservations herself. She'd imagined having him here in her room all week. She'd fantasized. She'd relived that night they'd shared on the Tahitian beach. But that kiss was still mind-bending.

Her head fell far back to accommodate it. His tongue did wickedly delicious things to her tongue, to the roof of her mouth, to every inch he could reach, convincing her that there was some merit to a man who had had as much experience as he'd had.

When he released her hand to wrap his arms around her, she found his shirtfront and tugged the tails from his trousers so she could finish the job she'd started.

Then, feeling a surprising lack of inhibition, she slipped her hands inside, to his flat stomach. She let her palms ride the rippling muscles of his washboard abs, upward to curve over his honed pectorals, rising to his expansive shoulders where she slid all the way over them and then down his biceps to shed him of shirt, tie and jacket at once, not caring that the finely made clothing landed on the floor behind him.

Then she kicked off her shoes and let herself have a moment of nothing but that kiss, the feel of his naked back beneath her hands, and his fingers working free the twelve tiny pearl buttons that traveled the length of her spine.

She thought it would take him longer than it did to get all the buttons open. Or maybe she was just so lost in his mouth over hers, in the tightening of her nipples in response to it, that she lost track. But suddenly she felt her dress loosen and Andrew slipping it off.

The bodice had a built-in bra and without the gown, Delia was left in only lace bikini pants and thigh-high nylons. And she wasn't about to be the only one of them that exposed. Especially not when she wanted Andrew equally rid of barriers. So as his hands massaged her back in a preview of what was to come, she went right for his waistband.

It made her smile to discover just how much he wanted her. In fact he was straining behind his zipper to such an extent that she had only to unfasten the hook at the top of it and that long, hard evidence did the rest of the work. From there it required only a nudge to send his pants to join the rest of his clothes.

Delia broke off their kiss to grin at him. "Am I mistaken or are there no Speedos?" she asked without glancing downward. Even though she wanted to.

Andrew grinned back at her. "Okay, so they're just boxers," he confessed. He began to trail kisses along the side of her neck. To her shoulder. Finding her breast even before the hand she'd anticipated, and sending a shockwave of pleasure through her as he divested himself of his own shoes and spun her around to ease her to the mattress.

Then he was gone.

Well, not actually gone, just not touching her or kissing her or doing any of those wonders with his mouth at her breast.

Instead he was standing above her, looking down at her as if he were absorbing every inch of her with his dark eyes.

Delia might have felt more self-conscious, but she was too enthralled by the sight he presented—magnificence personified in a body better than she'd even remembered, muscular, dynamic, perfectly proportioned.

His handsome face erupted into an appreciative smile and with his eyes holding hers, he rolled down her hose and followed them with her panties as Delia reached up to pull the pins from her hair and shake it free.

And then he was on the bed with her, partially beside her, partially on top of her, and it was as if everything broke free at once.

His hands and mouth were everywhere and so were hers. And between the fact that Delia had had no idea how alcohol-numbed she'd been that night in Tahiti, and the fact that hormones had apparently raised all her nerve endings closer to the surface of her skin, an entirely new array of sensations awaited her.

Every stroke of his fingers was intensified. Every kneading, sucking, flicking of her nipples was almost enough to send her right over the edge all by themselves. Every kiss, every trail of the tip of his tongue was a miracle unto itself.

It wasn't only what he was doing to her that took her step by step higher up the stairway of desire. The warmth and tautness of his skin was like French silk over steel, elevating her need to feel all the more of him. The bulge of each muscle was something to be explored, learned, reveled in. The tightness of each tendon, the power in each sinew, took her another step higher, inching toward what they were both striving for.

And the feel of that shaft when she reached for him, when she sheathed him in her hand, the sound of the deep, guttural groan that rumbled in his throat, the writhing he did in response, were all more heady than any martini she'd ever consumed.

Then, just when she needed it most, he was above her again, this time on the mattress, between her thighs, pulling her legs to wrap around his waist as he found his way inside her. Carefully. Gently insistent. Until he was embedded within her.

Slowly at first, they moved together. Rhythmically. As if they really were back on the beach, mimicking and maintaining the motion of the waves. Until bodies and needs demanded more, and Andrew began a quicker pace, a race up what remained of those stairs.

Delia kept up, her fingers digging into shoulder blades that seemed more than able to take it, meeting him and matching him, striving for that peak that came closer and closer and closer...

And then like heavy drapes thrown wide over a window at the top of the stairs, bright, brilliant sunshine flooded her and Delia reached the ultimate crest. She couldn't move with Andrew any longer, she could only cling to him as her body, her entire being succumbed to pure, exquisite ecstasy that held her in its velvet grip for one timeless moment of splendor.

Gliding down from that pinnacle when it had spent itself she discovered Andrew in the ending throes of his own climax. She felt him shudder slightly before he stiffened above her, within her. Like a glorious work of art, there he was, tensed and frozen for a moment of his own bliss.

When it had passed he also began the descent. It was as if the starch were being drained out of his muscles by slow increments. His hands were on either side of her head, his arms stretched straight, and as he relaxed he lowered himself to her, covering her with the welcome weight of his body melding itself to hers.

Then he pulsed inside her and reared up only enough so that he could kiss her forehead.

"Are you... Is everything okay? I swore I was going to be more in control just in case, but—"

"Everything is great," Delia assured him, laughing lightly at his concern.

He seemed relieved—and satisfied—because his supple mouth stretched into a cocky, lopsided grin before he dipped down to kiss her mouth.

Then he slipped out of her and rolled to his back, bringing her to lie at his side, wrapping her tightly in both arms to bring her close.

"So this marriage thing? Using a bed rather than a beach? Not so bad?" he asked.

"Not so bad," Delia confirmed as many, many things caught up with her and exhaustion began to take its turn. "What do you think?" she managed to ask.

"Better than not so bad," he said as if he meant it, sounding as worn out as she felt.

Too worn out to say more because Delia heard him exhale as fatigue overtook him, too.

She didn't have anything left herself to fight it, so after glancing one more time at the wedding ring on her finger, at her hand resting on her new husband's chest, she closed her eyes.

Drifting off to sleep with a warm, wonderful sense of security that she hoped would last forever.

Chapter Thirteen

"I'm on my way, Jack."

Andrew was rushing around the kitchen, trying to find his car keys when his cell phone rang. He and Delia had just said a lingering goodbye before she left for work and when the cell phone's display told him in advance that his caller was his brother, that was how he answered it, figuring Jack was annoyed that he was late.

"Tell me what day this is, Andrew," Jack ordered, his own temper clearly on the verge of erupting.

"Uh, I believe it's Thursday," Andrew said facetiously, peeved that his brother was being such a stickler. Again.

"Now tell me why it was important for you to get in here on time."

"Well, let's see," Andrew mused as he gave up on

finding his keys in the kitchen and moved into the living room to continue the search, drawing a blank as to what his brother was alluding to. "The reading of Dad's will is tomorrow, so that can't be why it was important for me to be there at the crack of dawn today. Was I supposed to bring breakfast or something?"

He heard his brother draw in an enraged breath and breathe it out through nostrils he imagined flaring.

"Right—tomorrow is the will reading," Jack said through what sounded like gritted teeth. "But today— *Thursday*—was the meeting with the Geltrace Chewing Gum people. The meeting that was to close the deal for us to do their advertising. The deal *you* were supposed to be here to close."

Andrew paused in scanning the living room to take his phone away from his face, throw his head back and mutter an expletive to the ceiling.

Then he brought his head down, put the phone back to his ear and started flinging sofa cushions out of the way in hopes that his keys had fallen from his pocket and lodged there.

"I forgot," he confessed. Because at that point, what else was he going to do but admit it.

"You forgot," Jack repeated.

"I've had other things on my mind, other things needing my attention." He didn't want to give details because the distractions all involved Delia and the fact that they hadn't been able to keep their hands off each other since the wedding on Saturday night. They'd both been leaving work early every day this week, spending most of their time in bed, and still hadn't been able to forfeit morning lovemaking in order to get to work on time each morning. Including this one.

But his brother didn't seem to care what his reason for missing the meeting had been, because from the minute he'd said that he'd had other things on his mind, Jack had been reading him the riot act.

And even though Andrew was only half paying attention, it was enough to make him angry. He was getting more and more sick of his brother as his boss.

Cutting Jack off, he said, "What happened with the gum guys? Did they walk or did you close the deal?"

"I shouldn't have had to close the deal. It was *your* deal. And David and I both had to dance around the client's doubts about just how trustworthy we are. Do you have any idea what it does to client relations when they show up, get led to a conference room and then have to sit on their thumbs waiting for the one person who's handling their account? Do you have any idea how David and I looked assuring them that you'd be here any minute and then finding out that the assistant we'd sent to try to reach you couldn't even get you on the phone? And why the hell *couldn't* we get you on the phone?"

"I didn't hear it. It was downstairs and I was upstairs," Andrew said, coming as near to the real reason he was late as he was going to.

"The client nearly walked out. David and I had to offer even more incentives to keep the account and all the while you were where? Sleeping in?"

Was his brother honestly that obtuse? Or was it just that Andrew's marriage to Delia was so completely a business arrangement to Jack that Jack couldn't fathom what *else* Andrew might have been doing upstairs and didn't see that he should be cut some slack to do it when he'd been denied a honeymoon in any other form?

Andrew's aggravation increased.

"We didn't lose the account so what's the point of this?" he demanded defiantly.

"We didn't lose the account but we could have!" Jack railed. "And we can't afford to lose anything. We can't afford to have word get out that George Hanson's playboy son lures clients in but may or may not show up to see the deal through."

Andrew had had it and he snapped.

"I'm not George Hanson's *playboy* son anymore, re-member?" he said, his voice loud. "As much as I'd like to be, you made sure *that* changed. So what else do you want from me?"

"More than I'm getting!"

"More? You want *more* from me? I sacrificed my whole personal life for the good of this company. I freaking got *married* so there wouldn't be any *more* ugly scandals to smudge the almighty Hanson name, the almighty Hanson Media Group. And if you think that postponing your big dreams of being a judge compare to that, you can think again. I'm sick and tired of taking what you've been dishing out even when I do everything you ask. So get off my back, Jack! Because if you don't, keep in mind that if I'm going to have to work for a living anyway. I can do that anywhere and for anyone—it doesn't have to be for Hanson Media Group and it doesn't have to be for you.

I can be someone else's *manpower.* And believe me, I'd rather be selling surfboards in Hawaii than selling advertising in Chicago."

With that Andrew turned off his phone, closed his eyes and tried to unclench his jaw.

Selling surfboards in Hawaii and never having to listen to his brother rag on him again—there was an appeal to that.

But after a few deep breaths Andrew calmed down, reminding himself that not showing up for that meeting this morning was a really bad thing to have done. Especially after having given his word to his client that he would *personally* see to it that they were taken care of to their satisfaction.

"Damn!" he said.

Shaking his head at his own screwup, he opened his eyes and spotted his car keys on the floor in front of the sofa.

Picking them up, he stormed out of the house, slamming the door behind him in anger as much at himself as at his brother.

And without any idea that he hadn't been alone in the house after all.

When the doorbell rang at ten o'clock that night Andrew spun from his path pacing the living room and ran for the entryway.

"Delia?" he said in a panic even before he had the door open.

But it wasn't Delia on the porch outside. It was Marta and Henry.

"Oh, tell me this isn't as bad as it looks," Andrew said, more to himself than to his new sister-in-law. "Is Delia all right?"

"She's fine," Marta said in a strangely clipped tone.

"Where is she?" Andrew demanded, ignoring it. "Has she been in an accident or something? She never came home. I've been calling the office, her cell phone—you guys—and when I couldn't get anybody, I even tried the police and the hospitals. I've been out of my mind worrying about her."

"She hasn't been in an accident," Marta said.

It occurred to Andrew only then that he should step out of the doorway and invite his in-laws in, so that was what he did, pushing the screen door open.

But neither Marta nor Henry took a step toward coming inside. Instead, Marta said, "I don't think so."

Andrew didn't have any idea what was going on but he was having some trouble feeling reassured. "Where's Delia?" he repeated.

"She's gone," Marta said flatly.

Andrew glanced at Henry where the other man stood partly behind his wife. Since Marta was being less than cooperative, Andrew was hoping to gain a little help from her husband. But Henry merely gave him the hard stare, offering no information himself.

So returning his gaze to Marta, Andrew said, "What do you mean Delia's gone?"

"She's gone," Marta said again. "And we've come to tell you that you're to get all your things out of here immediately."

"Is this a joke?" Andrew asked, wondering what else it could be.

"It's not a joke," Henry said. "Delia wants you out."

Andrew actually laughed a little. They had to be kidding. The last time he'd seen Delia was this morning when he'd lifted her onto the kitchen table where they'd shared not only a goodbye kiss but enough sexy groping and rubbing up against each other to delay both their departures for work another fifteen minutes before Delia had insisted they postpone what they'd begun until tonight.

But here it was tonight, and rather than having Delia back here, on the kitchen table, he was standing in the doorway facing her sister and brother-in-law, both of them looking stern and angry and disgusted. And for the life of him, Andrew didn't have any idea why that could be unless this was some kind of practical joke.

"Okay, I'll bite—why would Delia want me out of the house?" he asked.

"It's over, Andrew," Marta informed him in all seriousness. "The cat's out of the bag. She knows. We all know now."

"Know what?"

"That you're a liar. That you've been lying to her this whole time. That you didn't want to marry her or be a dad to the baby. That you only did it because your family made you."

"Delia heard you on the phone to your brother this morning," Henry supplied.

Andrew had had a day from hell even before coming home to spend the evening frantic and worried about his wife and he wasn't at first sure what Henry was talking about.

"On the phone to my brother this morning?" he reiterated, trying to think how that was possible. "Delia left before I did. Before I talked to Jack."

"No, she didn't," Marta said. "She went back upstairs to get her umbrella and you were talking—screaming at your brother—on her way back down the stairs. She heard the whole thing."

The whole thing? Andrew had been fighting with Jack all day. He had to mentally work his way backward to recall what he'd said on the phone that morning that Delia might have overheard.

But when he did that and remembered the gist of it, he knew he was in trouble. And he instantly felt even more rotten than he had moments earlier.

"Oh, man," he moaned, shaking his head.

"Kyle and I were the ones who talked her into giving you a chance," Marta said, unable to control her own rage any longer. "She'd have never let you get to her otherwise. She knew better. But Kyle and I both gave you the benefit of the doubt. Probably because we've had our own issues about fathers. Neither of us will ever forgive ourselves for this. For what you've done, you—"

"Just tell me where she is," Andrew said soberly, morosely.

"She's gone!" Marta shouted. "She's not even in Chicago so you can't get to her. And she's not coming back until you're out of here."

For the second time Andrew focused on Henry, hoping for any amount of help or understanding. "I need to talk to her. This is bad, I know. But—"

"I'm not telling you where she is, either," Henry said flatly, making it clear that there was no support from that quarter.

Marta seemed to have regained enough control to return to the cold, flat tone of voice again as she said, "Delia told me to tell you that she'll be contacting her lawyer on Monday. She'll ask if the marriage can be annulled but if it can't be, she'll file for divorce. She wants it quick and clean, she doesn't want anything from you, she doesn't expect anything from you. She'll go back to her original plan to have and raise the baby on her own, and you can tell your family that she won't even name you as the father so there won't be any kind of *scandal* to do damage to you or your business. No one will ever know the two of you even met, let alone that there's a baby." Marta seemed so furious she almost shuddered before she added, "And just for your information and the information of the rest of the big-deal Hansons? She would never have done anything that would have made any of you look bad or anything that would have hurt your precious dynasty. That isn't her style."

Andrew closed his eyes and shook his head, wondering when the hell things were going to get better instead of worse for once.

"This is all wrong...."

"I doubt if you even know the difference between right and wrong," Marta exploded again. "We're all hoping that you *do* go sell surfboards in Hawaii and keep your perpetual Peter Pan routine as far away from Delia as you can get! You might as well, you're free again, free as a bird—just the way you wanted to be all along."

Once again Henry contained his wife, this time with an arm around her shoulders before he said to Andrew, "Just get your stuff out of here and make yourself scarce. The least you owe Delia is to do whatever she wants from here on." Then he squeezed his wife and to her said, "We're done. Let's go home."

But Marta didn't leave without letting her eyes bore into Andrew a moment longer, her expression rife with disappointment and disillusionment that were harder for Andrew to take than anything she'd said in anger.

Then she allowed Henry to turn her around so he could take her to their car where it was parked at the curb, leaving Andrew with nothing but his marching orders.

He watched them go, still feeling a sense of disbelief that this was happening. But once Henry had closed the passenger door after Marta he shot another glance at Andrew and said, "Don't make this any uglier than you already have. Just get out."

Andrew didn't respond to that, he simply stepped aside so he could close his own door on the scene outside.

But he couldn't seem to move away from that spot once he had. He could only fall back against the heavy panel and slide to the floor, knees bent, elbows on each one, staring straight ahead at nothing in particular, and thinking, *Delia's gone. She knows and she's gone....*

It really had been one hell of a day. Worse even than that first day back from Tahiti when Jack and David had leveled their initial job ultimatum, and then he'd found out that same evening that Delia was pregnant.

Hanging up on Jack this morning had only made his brother more mad. They'd argued again at the office, to the point where David had had to step in. Then David had taken Jack's side and let Andrew know how he'd felt about Andrew missing the meeting with the chewing gum people. That had led to more shouting. More threats. More guff Andrew had ultimately had to take.

Then he'd come home to what he'd thought was going to be a night that would wipe away all the misery of the day only to find no Delia. To find himself increasingly terrified that something had happened to her.

And now this.

And even though the guilt—the almost intolerable remorse—he felt, he reached a point where he thought, *enough is enough.* How bad could selling surfboards in Hawaii be compared to all this? he asked himself. Sunny skies. Sandy beaches. No pressures. No responsibilities. So what if he didn't have a fraction of the money he'd always been used to? He also wouldn't have the rest of this garbage to deal with. He really would be free. Free as a bird—as Marta had said.

"Out of advertising. Out of the family mess. Out of the marriage," he told himself. "Say the hell with it all."

For a moment he thought he might do just that. He might go upstairs, pack his bags, and take off. Let Jack and David—and Evan, when he got there—deal with Hanson Media Group and all the problems, let them have whatever his father left, wash his hands of the whole damn thing.

And as for the baby? Delia could have that. She could have it and raise it exactly the way she was going to before they met up again by sheer coincidence. Exactly the way she'd decided she would when she'd opted not to even try to find out who or where he was to let him so much as know she was pregnant.

Life would go on without him. Everything and everyone would go on without him.

And he'd be free...

So why didn't it *feel* like he'd be free?

That seemed strange. Was it because he knew the family and the family company was in trouble and needed his help?

Was it because he knew now that there *was* a baby—*his* baby?

Did just knowing mean he'd never be free?

He thought about that and came to the reluctant conclusion that yes, it did. But there was more to it than simple knowledge not allowing him to be free of everything if he left it all behind, he realized as he analyzed it.

For the first time in his life, he felt the weight of his responsibilities. Now that he'd been in the trenches at Hanson Media Group, now that he'd begun to contribute to the family business—this morning's meeting notwithstanding—he could see how he could be of value. He wanted to be of value. And discovering that in himself made him realize that he couldn't simply turn his back and take off. It made him realize that the responsibilities and what he owed his family were real to him.

And so was his responsibility to Delia and the baby. *His* baby. *His* wife…

But it wasn't only the weight of the responsibilities that he felt, either. There was more than that when it came to both the job, and to Delia and the baby.

He'd liked the sense of accomplishment when he'd gotten that chewing gum account. He'd liked the challenge, the chase, and he'd liked succeeding when it had all paid off. He'd been as mad at himself all day as everyone else had been at him for missing that meeting this morning to close the deal, because he'd liked contributing something. Doing a job. Doing it well…

Well, doing it, anyway. Missing that meeting hadn't been doing the job well. But still, he'd done the job and he'd liked it. Liked that he'd been able to help the company by bringing much-needed business in, rather than only taking, taking, taking.

So yes, he'd had a truly lousy day at work and with his family, but no, he didn't want to turn his back on the job or Jack or David and take off.

But even more, he knew deep down, he didn't want to take off on Delia. That a big part of the job and the satisfaction he'd found in it was that it had made him feel worthy of her. It had made him feel equal to some of the things about her that he admired.

Because really, it was all about Delia.

He hadn't known that until tonight. Until he'd thought something might have happened to her. Until now, knowing that she'd left him, that she wanted him out of her life. But it was the truth.

Delia.

Pregnant or not pregnant, it was Delia who he thought about every minute of every day. Delia who he hadn't been able to wait to tell about the ad account. Delia who he couldn't wait to share even his smallest victories with. Delia who he wanted to be with to share everything.

He didn't know when it had happened or how. He only knew that it was the truth. That in the short time he'd known her, she'd become the most important thing to him.

Important enough to make him want to succeed at work. Important enough to make him want to meet all his responsibilities. Important enough to want to rush home to her every night, to be with her, more than he wanted to be on any beach in the world. Important enough to want to have this baby with her, to see what the two of them had created together, to be her partner in raising it and watching it grow and flourish into someone—with any luck—who would be as incredible as Delia was. Important enough to make him aggravated with his brother when Jack had acted as if his and Delia's marriage was nothing but a business arrangement when his marriage to Delia—no matter how he'd entered into it—was very, very real to him.

But Delia probably didn't know that. Not after hearing what he'd said to Jack on the phone this morning.

He wished he could turn back time and make it so that he hadn't said any of those things he never wanted her to know.

Things that had hurt her. Things that must have made her think of him in a way he didn't ever want her to think of him. Things that had caused her to leave him. To want him out of her house. Out of her life...

His elbows stayed on his knees but he raised his hands and dropped his head into them as if he had a horrible headache. When in fact, he had a horrible heartache.

"What the hell have you done?" he whispered to himself.

But he knew what he'd done. The real question was, could he fix it?

And how could he even begin to fix it when he didn't know where Delia was?

He'd never felt so low in his life. So hopeless. So rotten.

He had to see her.

He had to talk to her.

He had to get her back. To get everything back to where it had been before that damn phone call this morning....

Then something flashed through his head and he recalled Marta saying that Delia wasn't even in Chicago. But he knew Delia well enough to know that she wouldn't cut herself off from both of the people who had been her support system all her life. If she wasn't with her sister, she'd go to her brother. In California.

Andrew didn't have anything more than a hunch about that, but he trusted it. He had to. He had to have something to hang on to or he thought he might go out of his mind. Delia was in Los Angeles with Kyle, he just knew it.

And he could get there tonight if he took the next plane out.

But if he did that, his own family wouldn't be able to have the reading of his father's will tomorrow morning. The reading of the will that had been postponed for months now. That *needed* to be done. That left everything hanging in the balance until it *was* done.

Mending fences with Delia was Andrew's first concern, his first priority. A future with Delia made everything else worthwhile.

But there wouldn't be any "everything else" if he didn't at least stick around through tomorrow morning for the will reading, so he knew he had to do that.

The minute it was over, though, he would be on the first plane to California. To Delia, he promised himself. No matter what.

With the decision made, Andrew raised his head from his hands and tipped it back to the door, staring up at the steps in front of him, picturing Delia at the top of them, overhearing what he'd said to Jack this morning and actually feeling a wave of what she must have felt.

"Tomorrow," he said as if she were standing there now. "Just hold on until tomorrow when I can get to you."

But it wasn't only Delia who needed to hold on.

It was Andrew, too.

He needed to hold on and get through the hours until he *could* get to Delia.

He needed to hold on and just hope that he was going to be able to repair the damage he'd done....

Chapter Fourteen

In spite of the bombshell that had been dropped by his father's will, as the estate attorney left the conference room after the reading on Friday morning, Andrew checked his watch for the time. He had a plane to catch.

Luckily he wasn't scheduled to leave for the airport for another twenty minutes because the moment the lawyer was gone, his brother Evan revealed his displeasure in a snort of disgust.

"I'm so glad I came back here to be a part of this family again and do what I could for the business when I didn't get so much as a mention in the old man's will."

The omission of the middle son *had* been glaring.

"Why'd I bother?" he added.

"Please don't feel that way," Helen said, jumping in to console him. "We want you to be a part of the family, of the business."

"And you're in the position to say it, aren't you, Helen?" Jack said, obviously still reeling—as was everyone else—by the revelation that their father's trophy-wife had just inherited the controlling interest in Hanson Media Group. That as owner of fifty-one percent, they were all suddenly working for her.

"None of this has to be a negative," Helen insisted. "I've been honest and open with you, Jack and David about how much I want to be involved in the resuscitation of Hanson Media Group and now I really can be."

"The offices are already decorated, Helen," Andrew contributed wryly. Knowing his marriage was hanging in the balance had sent him into this meeting with little patience. What little there was had been stretched even thinner to learn that his barely tolerated stepmother would now be running things. Just when he'd thought it was difficult enough to be working under the jurisdiction of his uncle and brother, the situation became more difficult to tolerate.

The attractive Helen sat up straighter in her chair and leveled them all with an unwavering stare. "As a matter of fact, it was your father's wish that I stay out of the workforce as long as he was the breadwinner in the family. But I happen to have an MBA—"

"We don't really buy it," Andrew said.

"I also have ideas that none of you have given me

the chance to share," Helen insisted. "I can be more of an asset than you all realize."

"And now you have the power to *make* us all realize it, don't you?" Jack said.

Andrew couldn't blame his brother for being even more angry than he was about this turn of events. After all, everything Jack had left behind in his own life in order to take over the helm of Hanson Media Group since their father's death now seemed like a waste since he was working for Helen just like the rest of them.

"Please, can we call a truce?" Helen beseeched them. "Can we put the past behind us and simply work together as a family?"

"A family minus one," Evan said, his anger seeming to gain steam the more it sank in that he'd been over-looked by his father.

"We are *not* a family minus anyone," Helen said forcefully to the middle son. "And keep in mind that George may not have included you directly, Evan, but any kids you have will be in line for their share of the twenty percent interest in Hanson Media Group that's to be held in escrow for all Hanson grandchildren. And there was also nothing in the will that prevents you from working here, from holding just as high a position as any of the rest of us. That's something you and I can work out together."

"Can we?" Evan said facetiously, clearly leery of his stepmother's overture when the truth was that he and Helen had even less of a relationship with each other than Jack or Andrew had with her.

But Helen seemed determined to develop one now

because she met his sarcasm head on and said, "Yes, we can."

Andrew was surprised to see his brother's eyebrow arch as if Evan might actually be willing to hear her out at some point.

Then to the room in general Helen said, "I think we should look at this as a new beginning, not as something divisive. As a basic structure from which we can now all join together to rebuild Hanson Media Group for the benefit of every one of us and for the benefit of all the Hansons to come after us."

"She has a point," David finally chimed in after a prolonged lack of contribution. "Evan, I—"

"Yeah, yeah, yeah," Evan cut him off, pushing himself away from the conference table and abruptly getting to his feet. "I get it. Helen is in charge. She'll try to find something for the black sheep to do so we can all pretend that isn't what I am. I need some air," he concluded, storming out of the room.

"As I was saying," David continued, "I agree with Helen that we should look at the will as just a foundation to work from. Now we know where we stand, what we have to work with and we can proceed accordingly. Now we really can move forward. With Helen at the helm, but with none of us inconsequential."

"More than just not inconsequential," Helen was quick to amend. "Vital—every one of us in this room, and Evan, too, is vital to getting Hanson Media Group back on its feet. The bottom line is that we all just have to work together."

Andrew checked his watch again and with no more

time to spare, he stood. "That does seem to be the bottom line," he said, thinking that nothing—not even the prospect of working with his stepmother—was as important as getting to Delia. "And now I'm sorry to duck out, but I have some personal matters that have to be taken care of. I'll see you all on Monday."

Andrew expected Jack to jump on that, to question him, to demand that he work the day, to play the role of super-boss that he'd been playing since Andrew came on board.

But instead Jack pushed his chair away from the conference table and stood, as well. "To tell you the truth, little brother," he said with a sigh, "I think a three-day weekend is what I need, too." Then to their stepmother, he added, "I guess we'll see you here first thing next week, Helen."

Helen's expression was slightly forlorn and Andrew almost felt sorry for her.

But he had enough problems of his own to deal with. She'd just have to make her own way when it came to running Hanson Media Group.

It was eight o'clock Friday night when the doorbell rang at Kyle's and Janine's house in Los Angeles. Delia was finishing dinner cleanup with her nephew while Kyle and Janine went for donuts.

"I'll get it!" K.C. announced the minute the bell sounded, leaping off the chair he'd been standing on at the kitchen sink beside Delia in order to hand her plates to rinse and put in the dishwasher.

"Hold on," Delia called after him, grabbing a towel

to dry her hands before racing after her five-and-a-half-year-old nephew.

She reached the front door just as K.C. opened it.

Then she stopped cold.

Standing on the other side of the open portal was the last person on earth Delia wanted to see.

"It's that guy from your wedding, Aunt Dealie," K.C. told her without first greeting their visitor.

"Andrew," Delia said flatly, feeling a sudden resurgence of all the pain, all the disillusionment, all the embarrassment, all the disappointment, all the betrayal she'd felt since overhearing his phone conversation the morning before.

"Go away," she added when the feelings she'd been contending with and trying to keep at bay all washed through her.

"We need to talk," Andrew said, not bothering with a greeting either.

"No, we don't. I've heard what you *really* have to say. I don't need to hear anything else from you."

She also didn't need to see him looking the way he did. She didn't need to see those refined features, which any soap opera actor would have envied, tense and strained. She didn't need to see those dark, dark eyes that looked troubled now as they stared at her from above the faint bluish-gray hammocks left by no sleep. She didn't need to see the day's growth of beard that shadowed his sharp jawline and proved he hadn't been thinking about his appearance enough to shave. She didn't need to see the two vertical lines that formed from his brows pulled together, or the downward curve of his lips or the rumpled blue suit and less than crisp shirt he wore that were evidence that he'd been too distracted to pay attention to his clothes.

She just plain didn't need to see him. Or to feel—even amidst the awful things he'd just caused her to suffer again—the warmer, softer feelings that had grown for him since they'd reconnected, since they'd gotten married.

No, she definitely didn't need to feel *those* things….

After a moment of staring at her as hard as she was staring at him, Andrew altered his line of vision to take in K.C. instead.

"Hi there, buddy. I came to talk to your aunt. Think you can give us a minute alone?"

"This is his house. He doesn't have to go away, you do," Delia said before K.C. could answer, not wanting to lose her nephew as a chaperone. Or as a barrier between herself and Andrew.

"It's okay," K.C. said. "I can't have a donut unless I put away my puzzles, remember?"

And with that reminder, the little boy dashed around Delia and went down the hallway of the ranch-style house to his room, leaving her without a buffer.

But that didn't mean she was any more eager to be with Andrew.

"Please go," she said firmly, taking the edge of the open door in hand, making it obvious she intended to close it.

But Andrew crossed the threshold before she could, making it necessary for her to step out of his way.

"I'm not going anywhere," he said. "Not before we talk."

"I don't have anything to say to you."

"But I have plenty to say to you," he countered, taking the door from her grip to close it behind him.

Delia backed farther away from him. As far away as she could get before she came up against the archway that separated the entry from the Spanish-style sunken living room of her brother's home. But it felt good to have the bolster of the wall bracing her spine so she stayed put.

Andrew didn't come any closer, apparently getting the message that he needed to keep his distance. He merely stood in the center of the entry, tall and broad-shouldered, handsome and haggard at once.

"I know that you heard what I said to Jack yesterday morning on the phone," Andrew said then, cutting to the chase. "And I know it must have sounded bad—"

"It must have sounded bad?" she repeated. "It *sounded* like what it was—the truth. And yes, bad. Really, really bad."

"It wasn't the truth—"

"It wasn't?" she said, cutting him off again. "It wasn't the truth that you gave up your *playboy* status and life-style against your will? It wasn't the truth that you had this marriage shoved down your throat? That you were *forced* to marry me? That you sacrificed your personal life for your family's company to avoid more scandal? It wasn't—isn't—the truth that you would rather be on a beach in Hawaii than chained to me in Chicago?"

"No, it wasn't and isn't the truth."

"I don't know what's worse—that you're here because your family made you do this, too, or that you're still willing to stand there, look me in the eye, and go on lying to me."

"My family doesn't even know I'm here."

"Because you didn't want to tell them that you blew your cover and I left you because of it? You're hoping to mend fences before they find out?" Delia said snidely.

"My family doesn't know I'm here because it wasn't any of their damn business," Andrew answered.

"Oh, I don't know, since this marriage was a business arrangement it seems to me that that's exactly what it is. In fact, that's about *all* it is—part of the family plan for the family business."

Andrew closed his eyes and shook his head.

When he stopped and opened his eyes again, he said, "What I said to Jack came out of being mad at him and at myself. It was dumb. It was stupid. It was—"

"All the truth."

"Okay, yes, it was all the truth. But only at first."

That sounded too heartfelt not to be honest and Delia couldn't bring herself to refute it this time so she didn't. She merely stared at him, waiting for him to go on, torn between being glad he was dropping the façade and being struck yet another blow to hear that what he'd said the morning before really had all been the truth at *any* time.

When he did continue he told her about the pressures his brother and uncle had put on him to do the right thing by her, to marry her. He admitted that that might not have been the route he would have taken initially without their insistence.

"But the only thing that actually got me down the aisle was thinking about you," he said then. "Not that I realized what that meant last Saturday, but I came home after work yesterday and spent too many hours scared to death that something had happened to you to explain why you were never getting home, and then Marta and Henry showed up and told me why, and after another flirt with thoughts of flight, it all came together for me."

More thoughts of flight...

That stuck in Delia's mind as he went on to tell her about going from those thoughts to the rest of what had gone through his head both about his work and about her.

"That's when it occurred to me, Delia, that thinking about you to get myself down the aisle was only the beginning. That I've spent this past week wanting to get home to you. Wanting to see you, to spend every minute I could with you. Wanting to share my fledgling successes with you. Wanting to do everything, share everything, with you. And not because my family *made* me. Only because of the way I feel when I'm with you. The way you make me feel. I realized that pregnant or not pregnant, family pressures or no family pressures, you're the best thing that's ever happened to me. You're who I want. Being married to you is what I want."

Delia's eyes filled with tears she wouldn't allow to fall. But they weren't happy tears. Because as she looked at him, as she listened to him say words she could only wish to believe, she knew two things.

First, she knew that he'd made a strong case for her to marry him based on sentiments much like what he'd just relayed. But he'd already admitted that that had been something he likely wouldn't have done at all if not for his family forcing him to. Which meant that regardless of how convincing it had been, it had been an act. Just as this could well be.

And second, she knew that he was young and hadn't been ready to settle down. That she'd been right about him early on when she'd seen that vast difference in where they both were in their lives. When she'd told him that while she was at a place in time where having this baby, becoming a parent, were things she could embrace, he wasn't at that same place in time.

So she merely shook her head no.

It clearly wasn't something Andrew wanted to accept because his voice gained strength and frustration echoed when he said, "I'm telling you that the responsibilities are real to me now, Delia. The responsibilities to my family and the business, to you, to the baby. That they're as real to me as if they actually were things I was carrying around on my shoulders. And I'm not only willing to meet them, it feels *good* to meet them. To take them on. To know I can handle them, that I can be more, do more, contribute and take care of what I should be taking care of—"

"That has the ring of burden to it," she pointed out the way it seemed to her. And she didn't want to be a burden any more than she wanted to be the wife he was unduly influenced to have.

"Okay, sure, it was all daunting at the start. But now that's not how it is. Now it's nice to be…" He let out a half laugh. "This sounds hokey, but it's nice to be a full-grown man instead of some kid who flies off to the beach of the moment whenever the going gets tough. It's as if I've had my eyes opened to the person I can be and I like that person a whole lot better than the person I was before."

"I'm happy for you," Delia said, meaning it.

"Then you'll come home to Chicago with me and we can go on the way we were before that damn phone call?"

She was genuinely happy that he'd achieved what he had. But that didn't change the situation for her. And for her, the situation was that this was a much younger man who was just now growing up because he had to, not because he was necessarily ready to or had chosen to. A much younger man who was reveling in his newfound ability to carry some weight.

But it was new to him. Too new to consider him stable or reliable in that role. And she couldn't bank her own future and the future of her baby on something like that. On someone who could very well, at any moment, decide that having responsibilities wasn't his cup of tea after all and abdicate them—as Marta's father had done despite even his feeble attempts to be some part of his daughter's life.

And Delia definitely couldn't trust her own future or her baby's future to Andrew when she couldn't get that phone call out of her mind—the words and the tone that had made it obvious how close to the surface was still that inclination to blow off everything and go back to the lifestyle he'd loved and only left because other people had forced him to.

So again Delia shook her head. Only this time she said, "No."

"No?" he parroted as if the answer confused him.

"I'm glad you've come to some sort of place where you can accept the changes in your life and try to make the best of them, but that still doesn't make a good basis for our being married. It isn't why I'd want you to be married to me or why—"

It was Andrew who cut off her words this time. "There's more," he said with a drop of his eyes to her middle.

"The baby isn't basis enough, either," Delia said quietly.

"I'm telling you that I want you, Delia! That *I want you*," he repeated more strongly.

But yet again she only shook her head.

"I'm in love with you!" he shouted then.

But to Delia it seemed like a last-ditch effort and it only brought more tears to her eyes. "Was that the big gun you were going to use if nothing else worked?"

He looked as if she'd hit him in a weak spot. And now it was Andrew who shook his head, whose eyes actually seemed more moist than they had a moment before. "It was the big gun I didn't want to trot out and have used to shoot me down if you didn't feel the same way. Which apparently you don't."

Then he turned and walked out.

And when the tears in Delia's eyes began to stream down her face she wasn't sure if they were from the hurt he'd caused her, or the hurt she'd caused him.

Chapter Fifteen

"Breakfast in bed?" Delia said on Saturday morning when her brother knocked on the guest room door and then came in with a plate and a glass of milk.

"Your share of the donuts from last night—one chocolate glaze and one cake with white frosting and chocolate sprinkles. And milk to dunk them in," Kyle answered, setting everything on her nightstand as Delia sat up against the headboard.

"What time is it?" she asked as she broke off a piece of the chocolate donut and tried to pretend she had an appetite for it when her stomach was still in too many knots to be hungry.

"It's a little after ten," Kyle informed her.

"I slept till after ten in the morning?" Delia asked

in astonishment. "I haven't done that since I was a teenager."

"You were up until four," he reminded, propping a hip on the edge of the mattress and settling in.

"So were you. And Janine."

Kyle and his wife had kept a miserable Delia company as she cried until her eyes ached and rehashed her entire relationship with Andrew down to the last detail. Several times.

"Janine is still sleeping," Kyle said. "K.C. got me up. But he's off on a playdate now and even though I probably should have let you go on snoozing, too, I wanted a few minutes alone with you. I have some things to say."

Her brother looked serious and reluctant to have this conversation, and that made Delia particularly curious. Ordinarily Kyle had no qualms about telling her anything.

"Okay," Delia agreed. "Shoot."

"Andrew has called here four times already this morning."

Just the mention of Andrew's name made Delia drag her legs up so that her knees were almost to her chin. Then she wrapped her arms around the tent formed by the sheet and blanket, hugging her shins with both arms as if she needed protection.

"I hope you told him to go back to Chicago," she said.

"He called, asked to speak to you, I said you were sleeping and he hung up. Each time."

"So you *didn't* tell him to go back to Chicago."

"No, I didn't," Kyle said firmly. Then he glanced at the door he'd closed behind him when he'd come in, and said, "I've had Marta on the phone half a dozen times since Thursday so I know she blames herself and me for encouraging you to give Andrew a chance. She thinks he should be shot or beaten with a blunt object or something equally as dramatic. And I listened to Janine do the girlfriend thing all last night, rallying 'round, supporting everything you said—"

"Without you saying much at all," Delia said, only realizing in retrospect that her brother had been unusually quiet.

"Without me saying much at all," Kyle confirmed. "It seemed like last night you needed that whole girl thing kind of support so I stayed out of it. But I'm not so sure support for the way you're thinking about all this is what you need for the long run. Or that Marta and I were wrong in the first place."

That surprised Delia.

It must have shown in her expression because before she said anything, Kyle continued. "Let's just say that I have a different perspective on this whole thing and I think you should hear it, too."

"The male perspective?"

"I don't think it's male or female. I just seem to be seeing some things that no one else is."

"Okay. Like what?"

"Well, like I keep wondering what you expected from this guy?"

Delia's eyebrows arched. "What I expected from Andrew? Nothing."

"I don't mean that the same way you do. I don't mean in the way of money or child support or something. I mean, what did you expect from him when it came to this whole situation and marriage and relationship? Did you think he wouldn't have any insecurities about it? Any doubts? Any misgivings? Any regrets? Because it seems like that's the direction you've been going and I think it's a mistake."

Delia's surprise was mounting. "So you think I was wrong to react the way I did when I heard him say what he said on the phone Thursday morning?"

"I don't think there is any right or wrong. Yeah, I think what he said was hard to hear. Yeah, it stinks to find out that his family pushed him into marrying you to avoid a scandal. But the way I see it, you and Andrew both have two things going on and they're close to being the same two things. Even though you keep saying you're at different places in life because of the age gap."

"We are at different places in life because of the age gap," Delia insisted.

"You're both in a marriage—a first marriage—that came out of unusual circumstances. Age has nothing to do with that. And I'm here to shed some light on the similarities rather than supporting the disparities."

"Okay," Delia said again, unable to conceal the fact that she wasn't particularly happy with where her brother was headed with this.

"Look," Kyle reasoned. "You and Andrew like each other, you're attracted to each other, you enjoy being together, there are feelings, undefined or not, but feelings for each other—that's the good side. The romantic side that everyone has been counting on to prevail, and it's true of you both."

Delia confirmed that with silence and a slight, negligent shrug of only one shoulder.

But Kyle was undaunted and went on. "But this whole thing hasn't run a common course. You hooked up in a one-night stand that produced a baby. You accidentally met again, did a whirlwind courtship and got married. That's bound to come with fears and worries and concerns and regrets and the occasional freak-out when that stuff comes to the surface—that's the bad side. The second thing that's going on. For *both* of you. You, Dealie, have had a lot of your own fears and worries and concerns. But you seem to think that yours are warranted and his aren't."

"You think I'm being unfair?"

"A little bit. This whole thing hasn't had the smoothest, most leisurely start—that's a given," Kyle continued. "But consider this—Andrew only threatened to take off. And he made the threat to his brother, not to you. You're the one who actually did it. You're the one who's ready to throw in the towel on everything because you overheard Andrew say some things that shouldn't have come as too much of a shock. Well, except for the family pressure part of it."

"Not an insubstantial part of it," Delia reminded. "The man married me because his family made him."

"Come on. They may have pushed him or twisted his arm, but do you really believe that if he hated you, hated the whole idea, he would have gone through with it? Because I don't. He could have done a lot of other, honorable things to make it work out for everyone. He could have made arrangements with you for child support and visitation and been father to the baby no matter what. He could have gotten you to agree to some kind of gag order to keep it quiet, if that's what it took to appease his family. Or he could have just said to hell with it all and literally gone to sell surfboards in Hawaii. But he didn't do any of that. And I think he didn't do any of that because of the side of him that's attracted to you and enjoys you and has feelings for you—and I'm betting he really does have feelings for you, that he loves you or he wouldn't have said that."

"He might have," Delia said, holding out because the more her brother talked, the more guilty she felt for her own part in this fiasco.

"He didn't," Kyle said definitively. "And I'll tell you something else. I don't believe that without some pretty potent things going on in you, you would have spent that night with him in Tahiti or let him sweep you off your feet in the short time since your paths have crossed again. And then there's been this last week when you've been on cloud nine every time I've talked to you, and Marta said you were late to work every morning, and left early every evening—has that all been a sign that you don't really like the guy?"

Just the thought of the way she'd spent the past week made Delia feel flushed and she couldn't bring herself to answer her brother's question.

"Actions speak louder than words," Kyle said then. "And consider this—along with the fact that it was you who bolted, you gave Andrew his own easy out. You left Chicago, you said you'd get an annulment or a divorce, that you wouldn't cause any more problems for Hanson Media Group. You left him scot-free. If that was what the guy wanted on any level, why did he chase you all the way here? Why did he take what you dished out last night and come back for more today? He had freedom in the palm of his hand and he didn't want it. So what it looks like to me is that it's really you running scared and regretting this more than it's Andrew."

Kyle reached a hand to the top of her head and ruffled her already sleep-tousled hair in true brotherly fashion. "It's all right if that's the case," he assured then. "I'm with you if knowing the truth behind this is too much to take and you've decided you want out. It just seems to me that there's more between you and Andrew than you're paying attention to. More that must be pretty intense to cause you to do things that you've never done before. And if there's really something there, maybe you shouldn't turn your back on it because you've had a freak-out of your own. Seems to me—"

Delia rolled her eyes at him. "A lot of things *seem to you* today."

Kyle grinned and went on anyway. "Seems to me that if you've gone the 'give the guy a chance' route, you should really give the guy a chance, and not just bail on him before he can bail on you the way Peaches's younger men all bailed on her and on us."

Delia flinched. "You think that's what I'm doing? A preemptive strike?"

Kyle shrugged this time. With both shoulders. "I'm not saying that Andrew hasn't given you cause. I'm just saying that unlike Peaches and her boy toys, you and Andrew might genuinely have something that could work." Kyle leaned forward to nudge her legs with his shoulder. "And forget the whole age difference. Like I said, you're both basically at the same place anyway."

"Tahiti, Chicago, now California," she grumbled. "Every time we're in the same place I get into trouble."

"Yeah, well, just don't blame the whole thing on the guy. You're in this, too," her brother cajoled teasingly, lightening the tone.

"I knew this was a 'boys sticking together' thing," she joked back as if he'd revealed himself.

Kyle sat up straight again. "Marta and Henry and Janine and I are with you no matter what—we just want you to be happy. But think it over. Seriously. And from more than your own perspective."

Delia's brother got up and left the room then.

When he was gone and she was alone behind the closed door again, Delia dropped her forehead to her knees.

Had she bolted from Andrew before he could bolt from her? Was she the one doing the running? she asked herself.

It certainly wasn't a thrill to find out that Andrew had married her—or even presented the idea of marriage to her—because his family had made him. But had she used that as her bail-out clause? Her excuse to put an end to the bad side of things that Kyle had talked about—to put an end to all her own fears and worries about their age difference, about marrying someone she hardly knew, about whether or not she and Andrew really could have a future together?

When she considered it, she thought she actually might have done just that.

Because she had to admit to herself what she hadn't told anyone else in the last two days—that there was a secret part of her that had felt relieved that the worst had happened right away, before she'd gotten in any deeper.

But she knew she was already in pretty deep because with the exception of that secret part of her that felt relieved—and it was a very small part of her—she'd been miserable since making her decision to end things with Andrew. To call the marriage quits. And she knew that that wouldn't be true if Kyle wasn't also right about the fact that she had more feelings for Andrew than she wanted to admit.

The kind of feelings Andrew had revealed to her, and she had thrown back in his face.

"What a mess," she muttered to herself.

But when she took her brother's advice and seriously and objectively thought about the way things had been between herself and Andrew—in Tahiti and since the minute they'd laid eyes on each other again—she couldn't deny that there honestly was something that drew them together. Something that was bigger than both of them. Something that ignored conventions. Something even more than the fact that they were having this baby.

She and Andrew connected. They clicked. No matterr what the difference was in their ages. No matter how uncommon were the circumstances that had brought them together. No matter how many worries and fears and concerns they each might be harboring. When they were in the other's company, when their eyes met, when their hands touched or their bodies even came close, everything else faded into insignificance.

And really, wasn't that what was important? That and the fact that somewhere along the way, genuine feelings had developed and grown?

"Feelings you threw in his face, you idiot," she repeated to herself, aloud this time, but suffering even greater guilt and remorse for it.

Because yes, she realized that whatever it was that connected her and Andrew was what mattered most. They were what meant the marriage should be given a chance to survive. They were what meant that the baby should be born into it, raised in it.

And that was really what she wanted. Andrew. A future with Andrew. Regardless of how scary that might be when the insecurities and worries and concerns cropped up.

It was Andrew she wanted. Andrew she needed. Andrew she craved and desired and honestly thought was worth weathering everything else to have....

And then something just awful occurred to her.

What if Kyle was wrong about the reason behind

Andrew's repeated phone calls? What if he was calling to say he was accepting her offer to give him his freedom? What if he was calling to say that he actually was flying off to Hawaii or somewhere even farther away?

Delia bolted upright. "Oh, you really could have blown it," she moaned.

But maybe even if Andrew was calling to tell her the worst, she could still get to him, tell him she was sorry, that she loved him, too. Maybe she could stop him before it was too late….

Chapter Sixteen

As Delia stood outside of Andrew's hotel room an hour later she was so tense she could feel her heart pounding. Kyle had called hotels and motels near his house until he'd learned where Andrew was staying and had relayed the information to her. But now that she was there, Delia was terrified that when Andrew opened the door, she'd discover that he was packing his bags to leave.

Her confidence wasn't boosted by the fact that he hadn't called again after the four times her brother had told her about when he'd come into the guest room to wake her up. That didn't seem like a good sign and only encouraged her thinking that Andrew was taking her up on her offer to cut him loose from the marriage.

But she'd never know for sure until she talked to

him, she told herself, and so she finally forced a timid knock on the hotel room door.

Then she waited. And waited.

The door never opened.

She knocked harder, hoping that Andrew just hadn't heard the first one. But when there was again no answer her fear that he'd already left her behind grew and in response she dropped her forehead to a spot just below the gold 1346 that labeled the room.

"Delia?"

Startled, she jumped back from the door at the sound of her name from down the hallway.

A quick glance in that direction proved that she wasn't imagining it—Andrew was coming toward her. Looking freshly shaved and great in a pair of jeans and a bright yellow polo shirt that accentuated his broad shoulders.

"You're still here," she said the first thing that popped into her head.

"Where else would I be?" he asked as he drew near and pulled out his room key.

Adrenaline only made her stress worse and Delia wished she hadn't said that. She didn't want to begin this by letting him know she thought he might have taken off for a faraway beach after all. It seemed like the wrong tone to set.

So thinking as fast as she could, she said, "I wasn't sure if you had to get back to Chicago right away or not."

Andrew opened the door and then waited for her to go in ahead of him.

He seemed calm. Calmer than he'd been the evening before. Delia was afraid that didn't bode well for her cause. Maybe now that he'd accepted that his freedom would be restored, he was no longer as intense as he'd been when he'd shown up at Kyle's house trying to salvage their marriage.

Even though that possibility made her feel all the more awkward, she didn't know what to do except precede him into the hotel room anyway.

"You're not wondering why I'm here?" she asked as he followed her in and closed the door behind them.

"I'm just glad you are," he answered quietly.

"So you can say thanks for letting you out of this?"

She couldn't believe she'd actually said what had flashed through her mind again. And she hated that not only had it come out so spontaneously, but that she sounded so small, so full of dread.

Andrew didn't respond immediately. He tossed his room key onto his unmade bed before he glanced back at her with a serious expression lining his features.

"No," he said as if he didn't have any idea where a question like that would have come from. "I made up my mind last night after licking my wounds that I wasn't leaving here without you. I just went downstairs to make sure I could have the room as long as I need it, and I came back to get the keys to the rental car so I could show up on your doorstep again."

"Not to tell me you were accepting the annulment—divorce?"

He shook his head. "I'm not letting you call it quits just because I said something stupid in the heat of a fight with my brother. That's not grounds for an annulment or a divorce." Then, on a lighter note, he added,

"I was going to try bringing flowers today, though, to see if that might help."

Apparently with age didn't necessarily come wisdom, Delia thought, feeling foolish for having been so ready to end everything over an eavesdropped phone call when Andrew was taking a more rational view of the situation.

"Would the flowers help?" he asked then. "Because I can still go downstairs and get them."

"No, I don't need flowers," she answered before quietly confiding what she hated going through her mind. "I just want not to feel like the ugly cousin your mother made you take to the prom. But I don't know if I can."

"Because of the forced marriage thing," he finished for her.

"You made me believe that getting married was what you wanted," she accused.

"Would you have married me if I had told you what was really going on behind the scenes?"

"No."

"Nobody would," he said as if he didn't think anyone should.

"And you wouldn't have married me *without* what was going on behind the scenes," she said, but it stabbed her even as she did.

"Maybe you could think of it like this," Andrew suggested. "We're at the first summer camp dance of the season. The boys are lined up against one wall across the rec room from the girls on the other wall, and no one will make the first move. But everyone knows that you and I kissed down by the campfire at the end of the last year, so my friends give me a shove away from the wall to put the wheels in motion. Now, I could balk and elbow my way back against the wall. Or I could cross the room—"

Which he did right then as if he were demonstrating, stopping only a scant foot in front of Delia where she'd ended up after going only far enough into the room to allow him to close the door.

Then he continued with his fictitious scenario. "'I'm nervous about it—scared out of my head, to be honest—but I cross the room. And once I'm standing right in front of you and I take a good, long look at you again, I do ask you to dance. Because in spite of the push I needed to get me off that wall, there you are. You're as beautiful as I remember you. As beautiful as you were in all my memories of the summer before, all my fantasies. You're as smart and fun to be with. You're an amazing, incredible person, and I want you every bit as much as I wanted you the year before at the campfire.'"

Delia had been reluctant to look him in the eye and, as a result, had been staring at his chest. But now she tilted her chin, looking up into his dark, piercing gaze as he said, "That's how this was. I picked you myself, if you'll recall. In Tahiti. Without any help from anyone. It wasn't as if my family put a personal ad in a newspaper and then told me I had to marry the one woman who answered it. And I think I would have come to the idea of marriage myself after the baby news had sunk in and I'd had some time with you again to hash through that, to get to know you. But to do it instantly? That took a nudge," he confessed. "Only a nudge, though, Delia. The baby business threw me for a loop—I'm not denying that—but it only took a little while of being with you, getting to know you, getting to know what a great person you are, to realize I wanted you myself. Like I said last night, that's what got me to the altar last week. Not my family."

"And if I tell you—or even sign some kind of legally binding contract—that I'll never reveal your paternity or cause a single shadow to be cast over you or any of the Hansons or Hanson Media Group to cause a scandal? Then what would you say?" she tested, because as much as she wanted to believe him, she was still afraid he might be doing this for reasons other than his own.

"I'm not going to let you hide that this is my baby. And this stopped being about my family or about Hanson Media Group a while ago. I really knew it had stopped being about anyone or anything but you and me on Thursday night when I was going out of my mind thinking something might have happened to you. I wasn't just saying it when I told you that I love you. I *do* love you. And I'll fight tooth and nail to keep you and this baby, even if it means a media scandal of its own. I'm not letting you or this baby go. Not now, not ever. And if you think about it, consider how we spent last week. Did any of that seem like it was family mandated?"

That made Delia smile involuntarily. They'd made love more times, in more places, with more urgency than any honeymooning couple she could imagine. The man hadn't been able to keep his hands off her any longer than she'd been able to keep hers off him. Because there genuinely was something overpowering between them. Something far stronger than any family mandates.

She couldn't deny it and if there were any doubts left in her after all he'd said, she had only to remind herself that she'd given him a way out—no strings or scandals attached—and he still hadn't taken it.

"Are you saying I'm stuck with you?" Delia managed to joke, feeling suddenly much better than she had since Thursday morning.

"Permanently," he confirmed. "Although I would like to hear you say that if this was last week at this time, you'd marry me all over again. In spite of my big mouth."

"It seems just the right size to me," she said with an innuendo-laden tone.

He reached for her then, pulling her into his arms and wrapping them tightly around her. "And here we are, within inches of a hotel bed...."

"Plus it's our one-week anniversary...." she contributed.

That was all the encouragement he needed to kiss her. A deep, reconnecting kiss that let Delia know he meant all he'd said, that he genuinely did want her. As much as she wanted him.

And even though it hadn't been long since they'd last made love, it was as if eons had passed because suddenly clothes were flying off—her sundress and sandal and panties, his shoes and socks and jeans and shirt—and they were on their way to the hotel bed with mouths still clinging together hungrily, with hands already exploring, seeking, finding and arousing by the time Andrew gently laid her on the mattress and joined her.

But despite his tenderness in getting her there, what erupted between them from that moment on was explosive. Needs, demands, desires ran hot. By then each knew what the other liked, what spots were sensitive, just the right amount of force, of finesse to use to build anticipation, eagerness, pleasure.

And neither of them held back. Instead, as if all inhibitions had been set free, they came together in a way even more powerful than they ever had before, culminating in a simultaneous, blindingly potent peak that left Delia feeling as if they had physically sealed once and for all the bond they'd formed under less than ideal circumstances. A bond they gave new life—just as they'd created new life that night on the beach.

Afterward, exhausted, spent, satisfied, Andrew held her close, stroking her arm from elbow to hand and back again where her wedding ring once again shimmered from her finger resting on his chest.

"I love you," Delia whispered then. "And I'm sorry for what I said to you last night when you said that to me."

Andrew squeezed her even tighter. "That *was* pretty tough to hear," he said. "But probably not as tough as what you heard from me."

"I'll forgive and forget if you will," she proposed.

"Done." He kissed the top of her head. "And you know why?"

"Why?"

"Because I really do love you."

"I really do love you, too," Delia repeated, kissing the masculine mound of one of his taut pectorals.

"And the age thing—I'd like it if you'd let go of that," he told her.

"Your reaction to what's happened since Thursday morning was more mature than mine was," she admitted. "I kind of decided when that occurred to me that maybe it was time to forget the age thing, too."

"Finally!" he shouted at the ceiling.

Then he let out a sigh that she recognized. It was what he did when he was relaxing for sleep.

But she was ready for a little of that herself and so she gave up the fight against the fatigue that had settled over her, too, and closed her eyes.

Their legs were entwined, their bodies rested together in the perfect meeting of curves and valleys, his chest was the best pillow she'd ever had, and as Delia reveled in that sublime comfort and let it all cushion and embrace her, she also took secret pleasure in knowing that Andrew would still be there when she opened her eyes again.

And that was when it struck her that paradise wasn't only an island in the South Pacific.

That right there in Andrew's arms she had her own private slice of it.

Her own private slice of paradise into which she would bring their baby.

A baby she had no doubt Andrew would be there to greet with her when she delivered it into the world. Just as she had no doubt he would be there for her from that moment on.

* * * * *

Don't miss the next installment of the new Special Edition continuity,

THE FAMILY BUSINESS

Black sheep Evan Hanson has returned home to Chicago and is working for his stepmother, Helen. But an encounter with an old flame—now his employee—brings painful memories to light. Will Evan face the truth and reunite with the woman he loves—or will he run from his feelings once again?

Find out in

FALLING FOR THE BOSS

by Elizabeth Harbison

Available April 2006,

wherever Silhouette Books are sold.

HARLEQUIN®

Nxt
TM

The
GOOD KIND
OF CRAZY

TANYA MICHAELS

A forty-something blushing bride?

Neely Mason never expected to walk down the aisle, but it's happening, and now her whole Southern family is in on the event. Can they all get through this wedding without killing each other? Because one thing's for sure, when it comes to sisters, *crazy* is a relative term.